ADDICOᴛ
and ...es

by

Mike Kelly

Print Origination
Ince Blundell, Formby
Merseyside

Other books by Mike Kelly
Merseyside Tales

Also available on tapes recorded by:
Preston & North Lancashire Blind Welfare Soc.

First Published in 1995
Print Origination
Ince Blundell Formby
Merseyside

ISBN 0 903348 50 0

Printed and bound by Cromwell Press Ltd Melksham Wilts

Dedication

I dedicate this book to Diane a daughter to be proud of

Acknowledgments

I wish to record my thanks to all the people who have supported me with their encouragement and advice during the course of my writing of this little book.

My special thanks goes to Michelle Timson who kindly typed the manuscript and to Tom Morley who put up with my changes of mind throughout and gave me encouragement when I most needed it.

Contents

ONLY MY DREAMS TO DREAM

Two score years to work my bones,
  Sit and think in the fading light,
To lay alone on a damp cold night.
  Dream the dreams that never begin,

Shadow on the wall in the flickering light,
  A hand on the cot beside the bed.
The river is still on a foggy night,
    the clang of the buoy as it moves
With the tide.

Where is my dream on the far Oceans' wide,
  You've left me to push and to bear,
Alone in the night.
  To cry out with pain,
In the stillness of the dawn,

Your hand on my cheek to comfort me please.
  A vision of you as the stars in the night,
You are here for moment, to warm my heart,
  And then you are gone.

Forsake the sea my body is weak,
  The days are long,
Where are you now my dream on the far Oceans' wide.
  The ebbing tide with the children have fled,

At last you comfort me now in perfect bliss,
  One summer and Autumn then you leave me,
Only my dreams to dream.

1

Georgie and Freddy Horatio Mariner

Georgie never liked school very much; but then school never liked him, but, nevertherless he was a good boy and fairly well mannered for his tender years.

He didn't spend much time living with his mother, most of the time he was with his grandmother, and this was in the days when grandmothers were known to have wisdom.

Georgies mother lived about 8 miles away in Bootle, whereas his grandmother lived in an area of Liverpool called Huyton.

So Georgie would sometimes be with his mother and brothers and sister, but most of the time he was with his grandmother.

Georgie knew well enough that he was hopeless at school as did

Georgie knew well enough that he was hopeless at school as did the teachers, they would make him sit at the back of the class so he would be out of the way. However, due to sitting at the back of the class, he was sometimes unable to hear all that was going on.

He knew his school work was not up to the standard expected, but then most of the other lads in his class where not much better than him so Georgie never felt out of place, also like most of the lads in his class he was never commended for his work, as a matter of fact Georgie could never recall any comment except complaint from the teachers, but he never really blamed them because he knew that there where far too many children in the class, and the teachers were fighting a losing battle to instill anything short of the absolute basics into any of the children.

The only thing that Georgie ever won at school was a bar of chocolate, it was a very big one not like the ones you could buy in the local shops. Somebody had given the chocolate to his teacher, probably one of the other lads fathers, because only someone who travelled abroad could have a bar of chocolate of that size it must have come from a foreign country possibly America.

Well anyway, Georgie won the bar of chocolate and of course all the other lads in his class wanted a share, so he shared it out between them and it was generally agreed that Georgie was great, this opinion lasted about as long as the chocolate.

When he got home from school after winning the chocolate

Georgie told his grandmother about the prize and she was pleased when he told her that he shared it with the other boys in his class.

Winning the bar of chocolate however didn't stop Georgie from `sagging' school, but he only ever `sagged' for half a day, never a full day, not like Freddy Horatio Mariner who would sag school whenever he could, Freddy was always getting the cane for `sagging', but it never seemed to bother him, at least he never showed it.

Freddys dad was a seaman, and the teacher said he would not make a good sailor like his father because he was always `sagging', but Freddy said he didn't care if he never went to sea.

Georgie liked Freddy Horatio Mariner because he always shared his sweets with him. Georgies grandmother never had much money, but Freddys father always had money when he came home from sea, not that it lasted very long, because he was always getting himself drunk, and Freddy said that his mother would go down his dads pockets when he came home drunk. When he put his pants on the next morning he would think he had spent all his money in the Pub the night before.

When Freddys dad ran out of money he would ask his wife to go and borrow some from a moneylender so he could go to the pub again, so Freddys mam would pretend to go to the moneylender then she would lend him some of his own money and he never did catch on that it was his own money that he was borrowing.

One day Georgie and Freddy Horatio Mariner were on their way to school together, and Georgie told Freddy that his grandmother was baking a cake for his ninth birthday and she had said that he could bring along some of his friends to a party. Freddy said that would be smashin, so now that its your birthday we can stay off school. "But thats `sagging'" said Georgie, "I know but it is your birthday, we can go to the Pierhead and see the ships coming in" said Freddy. "Me gran will find out and tell the teacher," said Georgie, "no one will find out because no one goes to the Pierhead during the week they only go at week-ends," said Freddy, "are ya sure," said Georgie, "yeh honest," said Freddy.

"We will have to get back home in time for my party", said Georgie, "don't worry we will be home in good time for your party", said a very confident Freddy.

So off they went to the Pierhead to see the ships, and on the way Freddy bought some sweets from Missie Murphy's shop.

"You've always got money, Freddy Horatio Mariner", said Georgie. "Well me dads a seaman" isn't he" said Freddy.

Georgie just looked at Freddy and kept quiet.

"Georgie why do you always call me Freddy Horatio Mariner"? said Freddy. "Well its your name isn't it", said Georgie, "yes but why can't you call me Freddy like every body else", said Freddy, "the teacher never calls you Freddy, she says, Freddy Horatio Mariner" so thats what I call you said Georgie.

"Oh I give up with you, Georgie", said Freddy with a look of disgust. The two nine year olds soon forgot about everything else as they set off on their journey to the Pierhead.

"Do you think we will see any ships when we get there",said Goergie "of course we will, its a well known fact they are always there", said Freddy.

"I hope me Gran docsn't find out about me not being at school" said Georgie, "she won't find out and, any way I keep te;lling you its your birthday isn't it, and who's going to tell her", continued Freddy.

The two boys wandered along quite aimlessly not altogether sure if they were walking in the right direction to the Pierhead. Freddy started to chase a flock of pigeons that had landed in front of him, he ran into them with his arms stretched out making a noise like an aeroplane and the birds hopped to one side as he came charging at them.

A man suddenly stopped them and said "what school do you two go to", Freddy looked up with a look of horror on his young face. And without waiting for an answer, the man repeated the question, looking straight at Georgie.

"St Mary's" replied Georgie with as muchy authority as he could muster in his voice, "then why aren't you at school".

"Because its Georgie's, birthday" replied Freddy, "I see, and what is your name", "his name is Freddy Horatio Mariner", said

Georgie, — "Oh and I suppose your name is Nelson", said the man —"no it's Georgie" replied Georgie with a pained expression on his face.

The next day when the boys went to school they were told to go and report to the headmaster "Come in" said the headmaster when the two boys knocked at the door. "I believe you two boys decided to take the afternoon away from school yesterday is that right" — "well it was Georgie`s birthday sir", — protested Freddy.

The headmaster looked angy, "Oh so is that a good enough reason for `sagging' school", the boys stood in silence, "right I will deal with both of you now — sit over there" he said, pointing to Georgie, "and next time I assure you you will think twice about `sagging' school", "but sir" Freddy protested once more, "it was Georgie's birthday".

"Well I have a little birthday present I wish to give to the pair of you, first you Freddy Horatio Mariner stand over by my desk".

The headmaster pushed Freddys face down on the desk, then the cane came crashing down across his buttocks, six times in rapid succession.

Freddy was yelling blue murder as he ran out of the headmasters office, like the devil himself was after him.

The headmaster then turned his attention to Georgie, "now what about you my lad". Poor Georgie was so terrified that the pee was running down his legs, the headmaster saw the pool getting wider on the polished floor. "Right my lad I see you have learned this lesson well, — now clear out."

The two boys went home from school; one, with a sore backside, and the other with dented pride. Freddy told his dad that it was Georgie's birthday thats why they `sagged' school, "I hope its not another lads birthday tomorrow ya daft sod he said landing him a smack, ya can't go `sagging' school every time somebody has a birthday", Freddy gave his dad a funny look, but kept his mouth shut in case he got another clout.

The two young friends met up on the way to school the next morning. "I don't want to go to school, me Gran is going to tell me uncle Barny," said Georgie, "well he wont kill ya will he," replied Freddy.

"I don't want to go to school either even though my dad gave me a right smack", Freddie protested", "I'll bet that hurt", said Georgie, "you bet your life it did" said Freddy, "well thats two smacks you've had, and I've had none" said Georgie. Freddy stayed silent unable to find the words to answer his young friend.

"I want to go home to my mams' said Georgie, "but she lives miles away in Bootle," said Freddy. "I know that but if you want to you can come with me" pleaded Georgie.

"Your afraid your uncle Barny will give you a hiding tonight" said Freddy, "no I'm not," said Georgie. Anyway I don't see why

I should have got the cane and you didn't, that's not fair, it was your birthday after all" said Freddy.

The two nine year olds continued to argue about the rights and wrongs of it Freddy blaming Georgie for `sagging', and Georgie accusing Freddy. And neither one prepared to admit that they never wanted to go back to school.

"We could walk to the Pierhead, and, when we get there I know the way to my mams house", said Georgie. "What do ya mean, I'm not going to your mams house you can go on your own," said an indignant Freddy, but after a short debate on the merits of going to Georgie's mams or going to school, Freddy and Georgie were soon on their way to Bootle via the Pierhead. Without a penny in their pockets the two little saggers started following the direction of the trams, in the hope that they would lead them to the Pierhead.

"Have you got any money Freddy Horatio Mariner", — "Freddy, — its Freddy, why can't ya call me Freddy like every body else, your the only one in the class who never says, Freddy and every time you call me, "Freddy Horatio Mariner" people stare at me. Georgie chose not to answer his young friend instead he pointed to the number 10 tram that was heading towards them. The double decker tram which had a horizontal advertisement for a well known brand of whisky, seemed to float along shaking like a large jelly, and the friction of the metal wheels against the iron tram lines gave out a steady rhythm that was pleasing to the ear as it trundled towards the

Pierhead.

"We could have been on that tram if we had some money," said Freddy as he pulled off his navy blue jacket allowing the faint breeze to engulf him, giving him some little comfort from the rays of the hot sun in a cloudless sky over the two boys.

"We've walked a long way Georgie", Freddy continued. "Yeh we have", replied Georgie. "Do ya wanna sit down for a bit". Freddy nodded in agreement. The boys sat with their backs against the front of a bakers shop, and Freddy pushed his navy blue jacket underneath him to ease the soreness that he was still feeling from the canning that had been given to him by his headmaster the day before.

Georgie's head turned towards the door of the shop, the smell of freshly baked bread and cakes gave his tummy a funny feeling.

"How much further is it to the Pierhead", Georgie, asked Freddy whilst pulling two sweets from the lining of his pocket. "I don't think its too far", said Georgie stuffing one of the two remaining sweets that looked remakably like little hairy creatures into his mouth.

"Are ya sure its not a long way." insisted Freddy. "Well I don't think it is" said Georgie on the defensive.

"Me mam makes 'scouse' and she will give you some when we get to our house." "Whats that." Asked Freddy a puzzled expression on his young face. 'Its meat and potatoes and other things." said Georgie.

Freddy accepted Georgie's explanation of the meaning of 'scouse' and they set off on the long walk to Bootle, Freddy had dragged his jacket from the ground and told Georgie that his legs were tired and that they must have walked miles.

Georgie never answered but he too had discarded his jacket and allowed it to trail along the ground. The bright clear blue sky started to give way to dark gathering clouds as the afternoon moved on and the large buildings of the Pierhead came into sight. A cool breeze gathered pace and the temperature started to drop, and, as they looked up, the time on the face of the Liver building clock did not register as they walked in silence.

The wind and rain came from the river and drove into them as they quickly struggled into their jackets making them like wet blankets. The wind gave them no quarter dragging their little bodies from side to side as they struggled to stay upright, as they reached the open space in front of the Liver building.

"Over there, look Freddy Horatio Mariner, look there it is, its the number seventeen tram if we watch which way it goes out, we can follow the lines to Bootle". said Georgie on reaching the safety of the tram shelter.

"You're daft Georgie, there's tram lines running every everywhere". "Honest Freddy when we see the tram go out I'll know the way, because this is the way me Gran takes me to my Mams."

The two rain soaked and dejected boys now set off on the second leg of their journey, their feet squelching in sodden shoes and woollen socks which had gathered around their ankles in a crumpled mass adding to the misery that had over taken them. Georgie's eyes kept searching through the blinding rain for some sort of landmark, at last he recognized a church on the far side of the road, he always looked out for this church when he was on the tram with his Gran. The church had no railings or grass around it, the stone front of the church came out to the pavement, at that moment the voice of a woman called out to the boys from the gothic shaped doorway.

The boys ran across the road to the woman and into the shelter of the doorway. The woman looked at the pitiful sight before her and asked them why they weren't at school. Freddy looked at the woman and froze, he could see the sight of the headmasters cane towering above his head.

"We've been to the Pierhead to see the ships." replied Freddy hoping his explanation would do the trick. The woman smiled at the two boys and gave them each a sweet. "What's your name", she said. "My name is Georgie and this is Freddy Horatio Mariner". "Freddy who". said the woman, "Oh I see Freddy that's a nice name, now you wait here and I will put you on the tram when it comes." continued the woman.

The woman put the two boys on the first tram that came along and told the conductor just where to put them off. When they arrived at their destination the boys walked along the street towards Georgie's house the rain still beating down on their heads. Georgie pushed open the unlocked front door and walked in to the smell of cooking sausages and in the grate was a roaring fire, its warm glow engulfed Georgie and Freddy.

Georgie's mother walked into the living room when she heard the boys enter. "Oh my God," where did you two come from, you look like drowned rats, who's that, her eyes fixed on Freddy. "Its Freddy Horatio Mariner he goes to school with me." "Doesn't look like he's been to school with you today, you had better sit down and we will sort things out later. Freddy smiled at Georgie when he saw the two plates of sausages. Eat them up then we'll decide what we will do with the pair of ya'.

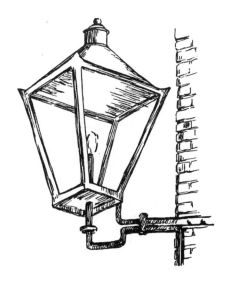

Street Gas Lamp

17

A view of the Liverpool Landing Stage c. 1919

My Dilemma

I arrived in Dublin at about nine o'clock on a Tuesday morning intending to stay for three days, it was a last minute decision. The flight from Liverpool took about half an hour. I had nowhere to stay, but I felt that would not be a problem, I thought I would soon find a place. When I arrived in the city however I had a rude awakening; tourists were everywhere, and then I realised it was the first week in August and tourists always abound. I made my way to Bewley's cafe in Westmorland Street for a bite to eat and to do a little thinking.

After eating, my energy level had risen somewhat and my task was now to find somewhere to stay, that however proved to be no easy matter and to add to my anxiety it had started to rain. It started just as I stepped out onto the pavement with my little shoulder bag containing a clean shirt, a pair of underpants, one pair of socks and a toothbrush; I am nothing, if not well prepared when I go away for a few days.

The rain continued like a spluttering, dripping tap, as I made my way in search of somewhere to stay and the more I walked, the more the tap seemed to be turned on. I didn't have an umbrella or cap so the dancing rain played a rhythm on my bald head. I was starting to look a sorry sight in my quest to find a bed for the night. I tried a number of places, even the youth hostels, the answer was always the same, `Sorry, we are full up.'

Not being in the big league, I could not afford the price of one of the larger hotels, and I was getting to the stage where paranoia was setting in, but then, some of my friends say I'm that way already and I suppose I have to face the fact that I must be out of my head, for who in his right mind would go to Dublin the first week in August without making arrangements for somewhere to stay.

At last I thought I'm in luck I came across a small hotel with a sign in the window which read 'Vacancies'. I stepped into the porch and rang the bell alongside the glass door covering the porch into the hallway.

The sound of the bell attracted the attention of a pleasant young woman who was coming towards me along the passage behind the glass door. Have I cracked it? Am I on? Is this smiling young woman going to say `Yes, We have a room.' She turned the key on her side of the door and her smile grew wider, I returned the smile ready to move forward, my mouth open ready to plead for sanctuary, but the smiling young woman got in first.

' Sorry, but we are full up.'

`But the sign ..' I stuttered.

`Oh! Yes,' she continued, `I forgot to take it down,' the smile still on her face.

I turned to leave as the excuses kept coming from her and the paranoia was really starting to build up, and off I went feeling very sorry for myself. Then out of the clear sky came the sunshine, The rain had gone and across the street in big bold letters `BARRY'S HOTEL.' I ran towards it, well not quite ran but I certainly quickened my pace.

`Have you got a room for three nights? `I asked the young woman who looked up at me from behind the desk, not a smile on her face.

`Yes, we can let you have a room on the first floor, `en suite.'

I accepted the offer and went straight upstairs to the room and unpacked my bag taking out my sparce belongings, then lay back on the bed. `To think I have my own bath room. Good old Dublin, I knew you wouldn't let me down.' I thought to myself as the paranoia was subsiding.

Well, now that the roof over my head was secure and I didn't have to look up at the stars lying on a park bench, I set off for a walk down O'Connell Street and once more made for Bewley's Cafe to sit in wonderment at all the people that keep this cafe busy all day long. It's more than a place to have a cuppa or a meal, young and old alike love to sit in this world of charm.

After my meal, I set out for `Dublin Writers `Museum and what a joy it was. I felt like a peeping Tom. Looking through the window into the private world of those wonderful Irish writers, but then I don't suppose there is such a place as a private world for a writer he is as exposed and naked as the first seconds of his birth, and if I was an intruder into their personal lives, at least I know a little more about them and it is as they intended. James Joyce, that all embracing artist, his words strike out at you and hold you in their embrace, like Michael Angelo's images.

Sean O'Casey is another of my favourite writers and Liam O'Flaherty, but the darling of them all is Brendan Behan. Maybe it's because of his working class background, although some have tried to dispute his working class connections.

Brendan had afterall a brief encounter with another town I love so well; Liverpool, then after taking in all this intellectual nourishment at the museum I then decided to sample the flavour of the local Pubs.

The following morning after a good nights sleep I joined the thousands of tourists who had come to old Dublin City. It was a bright and sunny day and everybody seemed to be in a happy mood no one more so than myself, the joyous atmosphere had put a spring in my step and my legs felt that they were free from the worry of obtaining the room last night.

I thought I would go and look at the fruit market at the back of O'Connell Street, but first I had to enter Henry Street, and join the hundreds of shoppers who filled this pedestrian highway. I had the felling I was on a large chess board taking up the length and width of the street with too many chess pieces and nowhere to move, and there I was, a pawn, only too happy to take part in this crazy game. A move could only take place when somebody moved sideways or if they disappeared into one of the many shops that run the full length of the street. It was great to wander from one side of the street to the other, moves permitting of course, without worrying about motor cars tearing past you.

In many ways it was a nice feeling moving with a large mass of people, and at one stage my mind got carried away as I ploughed my way through the street, I seemed now to be taking part in a gigantic musical. The buskers lined each side of the thoroughfare, playing everything from classical to pop music, and all waiting their cue from the director before the whole mass of people burst into song.

To the right of me was Moore street housing the fruit and fish stalls. The whole area was filled with people buying and selling, and the women who attended the stalls were overflowing with their wonderful sense of humour. It takes someone with a sense of humour to be able to stand there in the winter months, however, this was summertime and the air was filled with laughter even if money was hard to come by.

Molly Malone will never be dead, `Or die of the fever.' As the song goes, while we have the women at the entrance to Moore street pushing their old battered prams with a wooden tray on top, displaying a variety of wares, anything from oranges and lemons, to what ever else was available they could to sell to keep body and soul together. The whole of this area is a cavalcade of colour, a kaleidoscope of people, the good, the bad, the mighty and the poor. This great open air theatre goes on for six days a week, only coming to rest on a Sunday when the lights are turned down and silence hits the stage.

I leave Henry street with Moore street behind me, taking no more part in this ceaseless show and make my way once more to Bewleys cafe for a much needed cup of coffee and a chance to rest my weary feet. After my coffee and a bacon butty, I step out once more into the milling crowd of tourists, who, like my self, never seem to know where they are going.

After strolling for some time in the sunshine amusing myself looking at the tourists in Grafton Street I make my way to the Abbey Theatre where the name George Bernard Shaw is displayed, it stopped me in my tracks. I stood taking in all the information on the posters hanging on to every word, much the same way I did when I was a teenager.

The last time I saw a play from the great man himself was `John Bull's Other Island `at the Gaiety Theatre years ago, so I thought I would treat myself once more. The young man at the booking office said: I have a seat in the front stalls close to the stage.' Somehow I got the feeling that the man thought I was a bit deaf, well of course he was right, my years working in the ship yard had taken its toll. I smiled at him. `Yes that will do me fine, a seat near the stage.' `Please try to be early the performance starts at eight o`clock prompt.' said the young man.

Walking back towards O`Connell Street clutching my ticket to see another play written by George Bernard Shaw, I felt like a man who had just won a fortrune at the local bingo hall. So to celebrate I made for the first bar that came in sight before I set out for my digs to prepare my self for my night of culture.

After quenching my thirst, I left the bar, but on the way out I caught my wrist watch, strap on the door and my watch went flying across the pavement. As it was only a cheap battery driven watch I picked up the scattered pieces and deposited them in the a rubbish bin on the edge of the pavement.

In my haste to get ready, I turned on the television in my room to get the time, and the digital clock on the screen showed that I had better get a move on, so off I went at fifteen minutes past seven according to the time on the television screen. Making sure I still had my precious theatre ticket in my pocket, I jumped on to the first bus that came along. I asked the driver if he went anywhere near the Abbey Theatre, he nodded in a sort of polite way without looking at me. I'll give you a shout where to get off.' he said. I then placed a pound coin on the tray in front of the driver, but he refused to take the money and indicated that I sit down. I accepted the man's kindness gracefully and sat down thinking this is a nice way to start an evening at the theatre.

When I arrived at the Abbey, an attendant was standing at the main entrance and I asked him if the bar was open, as I felt like having an orange juice before taking my seat in the auditorium. The man looked at me the way you look at an idiot, when they ask you a question for which you have no answer. I moved forward towards the foyer while I was waiting for his answer, but he stopped me in my tracks. `The bar is closed until seven o'clock.' said the man trying to hide a grin. Then, I thought, what bloody time is it now?. I did not have the nerve to ask the man the time, I was starting to feel like the idiot that he must have thought I was.

To calm myself down, and to regain my composure, I headed for a bar along the street and ordered a whisky to steady my nerves and, hopefully wipe away the foolish look on my face. When the barman placed the whisky in front of me, I asked him in the most casual way I could what time it was.

`It's just forty five minutes past four o'clock,' said the man.

I just kept repeating the time to myself in disbelief.

This was priceless wasn't it, here I was more than 2 hours behind the time I thought it was I was suely in the middle of my own dilemma, and to think I was going to see George Bernard Shaw's `**The Doctor's Dilemma**'.

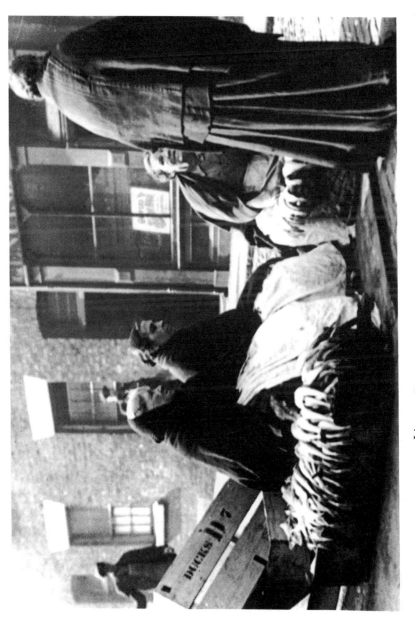

Liverpool's pavement fish sellers c. 1890

Liverpool's Wapping Dock in its heyday

3

Curly Murphy

Curly Murphy had always kept chickens in his back yard for as long as any one could remember. No one seemed to mind when the cock crowed in the early hours of the morning, because most people had to be up early to get to work on the docks. However, Sunday morning was an exception and people expected to have an extra hour in bed, before getting up to put the salt fish simmering on the gas stove before going off to church, the fish was always left on a low light.

By the time they got back from church, the house would reek with the smell of the fish, and the taste buds would be brought to a peak with anticipation all waiting for a breakfast of salt fish, so Curlys crowing cock would never win any popularity contest on a Sunday morning.

The chickens had the run of the small back yard, but sometimes they too were a nuisance getting under Curlys feet when he wanted to go to the lavatory at the bottom of the yard. Curly was a tall man with big hands and flat feet and a pale complexion due to him not seeing much sun light working in a warehouse in the docks, so I suppose his hobby of keeping chickens was a good way to get some fresh air into his lungs and a way to make a few shillings from selling eggs to his neighbours to augment his meagre wages.

He knew his neighbours would never risk much abuse about his cock crowing on a Sunday morning otherwise they may be deprived of the cheap eggs from the chickens in his back yard.

Curly was a gentle sort of man and his only adversaries were the cats that stalked his back yard walls, he was well able to keep them at bay with the help of the little scots terrier, that the foreman in the warehouse had given him. The foreman's wife was not too keen on dogs, and he knew that by giving the dog to Curly it would have a good home, and Curly would no doubt show his appreciation by giving the foreman some of his fresh eggs

Curly being the gentle man that he was, never looked forward to the build up towards Xmas, because that was the time he had to think about fattening up some of his older birds for the roasting dish, if he was to do right by his neighbours But culling the chickens for the festive season, always created a great problem for his mind, He himself could never carry out the coup de grâce on his little feathered friends and this particular Xmas Curly was having great difficulty in finding someone to carry out this decidedly unwanted chore. However Curly was not to be out done. He had in mind two young lads, who lived only a few doors away. So away he went and asked the boys father if his two young sons could play the part of executioner.

Kevin was the older of the two boys by twelve months, he was a strong for a fourteen year old, with broad shoulder's. Brian was the quieter of the two, but he was as tall as Kevin, and it was plain to see they were going to be two fine big men in a few years time.

`Sure they will help you out. 'Said the boys father, without consulting the young lads. `I'll give them, ten shillings if they will ring the necks of ten of my hens.' Said Curly, the words nearly choking him as they left his lips. By this time the lads had joined their father at the front door and were looking at Curly in disbelief.

`We have never killed chickens.' stammered Kevin. Brian not saying a word. Go on lads have a go. Said their father trying to prompt them, but the boys never answered.

`Well would you like to kill them for me.' said Curly looking at the boys father, `Well er no, I would sooner leave it to the boys, it will be a bit of pocket money for them. The boys looked at their father with a look of submission on their young faces.

`O,K, we will do it said Kevin, looking at Brian, the boys father looked please with himself knowing that he did not have to do the dirty deed.

Curly led the boys to the chosen place of execution in the basement of his house, the boys father declined the offer of watching his sons carrying out the task. The chickens chosen to fill the roasting tins for the festive season had already been selected by Curly, and were pecking away on the basement floor having their last supper. Do you know what to do, Curly asked the boys, they gave no answer, Brian stood with his back to the white washed wall his lips were sealed on looking up at Curly.

`I don't know what to do.' said the more daring Kevin,` I've never killed a chicken before', he continued. 'Its easy' said Curly. `Your scared' came a sharp reply from Brian. No I'm not its just that I don't like killing my own chickens. `Shut up Brian, and seeing that you have a lot to say you can kill the first five, and I will kill the rest of them'. `No you be the first your older than me 'said Brian his back pushed closer to the wall, then he let out a sharp yelp like a pup as a one of the chickens brushed against his legs.

`Alright I will do the first five, but I don't know what to do cried Kevin. `Oh its easy, said Curly, you sit on that chair over there, then you get one of the chickens and put it between your knee's, Kevin looked up at Curly the fear of the unknown starting to grip him as he made his way to the chair reluctantly he sat down. `You will have to get hold of one of the chickens first, they wont come to you, then press your knee's tight to hold it.

`Then why don't you do it if you know how,' Curly, said Brian with a grin on his face, Curly chose not to answer.

Kevin leaped onto the floor grabbing one of the birds by the leg, the rest of them scattered in fear of their lives, whilst Kevin pulled the screeching bird back to the chair. The remaining birds gathered in the far corner, and Brian still kept close to the wall, a look of fear covered his countenance, and satisfaction spread over the face of Curly, knowing that the task was about to be carried out. Kevin sat with the bird between his knee's awaiting further instructions. `Pull its wings down by its side then press your knee's tight against its side, then put your two hands around its neck, and twist, its easy.'

`If its that easy, why don't you do it, instead of getting our kid to do it. 'Said Brian, his back still holding the wall up. Kevin looked towards Brian as he tightened his grip around the neck of the chicken, Brian put his hands to his face shielding his eyes from the scene unfolding before him.

A silence descended on the basement, and, strange as it seemed, the rest of the hens didn't seem to be the slightest bit bothered by what was going on and continued to peck away at scraps on the floor.

Kevin twisted the neck of the chicken like twisting the top off a bottle, the head came away in Kevin's strong hands and he dropped it onto floor and as he loosened his grip on the headless bird it ran around the basement then slumped at the feet of the terrified Curly who tried not to show his fear.

The booming voice of the boys father broke the silence. How are my courageous young fella's getting on, his fat frame leaning against the door, the boys didn't answered and Curly just gave a nod. The boys father looked at the headless chicken then started to give Kevin advice on how to do the job properly. `Would you like to show Kevin how its done dad, said Brian recovering from his ordeal. `Well er no like, I think Kevin's got the hang of it without me showing him.` What you mean dad, you and Curly are not scared to do it yourselves continued Brian. No its not like that, I'm thinking of you and Kevin getting the ten shillings, Isn't that right Curly. 'A nod of the head from Curly was the only gesture made.

Kevin reluctantly stepped forward to grab another chicken then settled back into the chair. This time Kevin was a little more composed, he had learned lessons from his first attempt. This time his hands applied only the necessary pressure and the bird fell silent at Kevin's feet. Curly his hands shaking removed the bird from the floor, and Brian was still glued to the wall awaiting his call to play the executioner, and the fear was building up inside of him as he watched his older brother become more professional in his task.

A silence filled the basement as Kevin got on with the job, the two men started feeling a bit uneasy allowing the boys to carry out the task that they would not do. The silence was finally broken by Brian. `Why don't you and Curly, have a go dad, or are you too scared. `Shut up Brian its bad enough doing this without listening to you going on, anyway it will soon be your turn. Said Kevin.

Silence filled the room once again as Kevin got into the swing of things, but his stomach seemed to be turning in knots, doing a deed he never imagined he would ever, have to carry out. One by one the chickens fell at his feet until the fifth one was removed by a sheepish looking Curly.

Kevin looked towards his younger brother and Brian looked back at Kevin with eyes wide open, he shouted out.` I'm not killing the other five let me dad do it. 'The boys father choose not to get involved in Brians outburst hoping they would sort it out themselves, Curly also remained quiet not wanting to get involved in family matters.

Brian might have been the younger of the two boys by one year, but he had more to say, he accused his father and Curly of being cowards, and the two men looked down at the floor, `Come on Brian its your turn.' Said Kevin. `No let me dad do it instead of watching us. `What do you mean I'm the one who is doing it, you haven't killed any of them, and if you don't kill any of them I will keep the ten shillings all for myself.'` Well you can do the rest seeing that your so good at killing chickens.

`Alright big mouth I will kill the rest of them but don't expect any of the money. 'Said Kevin who was by now in full control of what he was doing. `Any way your all cowards me dad, Curly, and you. 'Continued Kevin. And he felt as though he had been cheated in having to do the job all by himself and his stomach still felt funny, but he did not want to lose face in front of the rest of them. So Kevin continued with his grim task until all ten chickens had been slaughtered.

As Kevin got up from the chair Curly moved forward to hand the money to him for completing the task. Curly's foot caught the prostrate body of the last chicken to be killed its twitching form seemed to throw Itself at Curlys lower leg, Curly yelled with terror in his voice and as he collapsed in a heap the coins fell from his hands and scattered onto the floor of the basement. Kevin rushed forward to pick up the coins then handed half of them to his brother as the two boys looked back from the doorway with a smile on their faces to watch their father struggling to help Curly to his feet.

Street water tap

The Young Starling

An intermittent faint squeak seemed to come from the direction of the sandstone that was encircling the rockery that lay at the bottom of the garden. The faint sound attracted the attention of the seven year old boy as he walked out from his mums kitchen and into the garden. The young boys sharp hearing picked up the sound and its direction. He placed the bowl full of bread crumbs that his mother had given him to feed the birds that landed in the garden because it was spring and they needed all the energy that they could muster as they were still caring for their young chicks.

Jamie shoes were making too much noise on the gravel path so he moved onto the newly cut lawn and hunched his shoulders and bent his knees as he crept towards the rockery, his listening was intense in the hope that he would pick up the sound of the squawking again, just at that moment a young bird suddenly hopped from behind the rockery its flight feathers not fully formed, Jamie got a fright and jumped back startled, then he became brave upon realising what caused the noise and kneeling down in the grass and poked a finger at a young starling, well he thought it must be a starling because his mother kept pointing them out to him when they landed in the garden.

When they landed in the garden Jamie's mother would say `they are a nuisance those starlings, they come down and cover the lawn and perch all along the fence.' So he thought he had better not tell his mum in case she chased it away. As he pushed his finger towards the young bird, it moved its head back and opened its beak wide the way it would do when its mother was feeding it but the mother was nowhere about as Jamie looked up into the tree at the bottom of the garden.

He now tried reaching out to pick up the bird, but its nimble legs were too quick for him and it propelled itself across the lawn. Its young wings did not, as yet, have the strength to lift it off the grass, so it came to a sudden stop as though it had applied the the brakes. It was gasping for air and its little chest was pumping in and out like a bellows, the lack of nourishment seemed to be taking its toll. The young starling was not happy being so exposed on the open lawn, so it made its way between the thorny rose bushes.

The boy tried in vain to reach into the rose bushes but each time he caught the back of his hand on the thorns. Jamie felt a stinging sensation, and he let forth a blast of anger towards the young bird who by this time had moved further into the shelter of the rose bush.

Jamie continued to rub the back of his hand as the pain came in waves and each time he cried out he shouted at the bird to tell it that it was its fault for the suffering that he was experiencing. The young birds response was to put its head back and open its beak followed by a faint squeak trying to summon its mother but she was nowhere to be seen, and only the boy was responding to its distress call for help. `Bloody nuisance.' Jamie cried out still rubbing the back of his hand as he turned his back on the bird, and started to walk back to the house.

He looked back over his right shoulder towards the rose bushes thinking to himself, how ungrateful the young bird was. Then he stopped and turned once again towards the bird. `I only wanted to rescue you, daft bird, you can stay there, I hope the cats get you. 'Jamie continued his retreat into the house still rubbing his hand.

Out in the garden the young starling was still trying to attract attention by chirping and hopping about, but the lack of nourishment was now severe and soon the young bird came to a halt and sat still under the rose bush its energy exhausted.

Samson, the black cat from next door, had jumped up onto the six foot fence and was walking along the top with perfect balance its brain sending the right singles to every muscle in its body. Then the cat spotted the young starling sitting out in the open away from the security of the rose bush. he brought himself to a rigid halt his head protruding straight out from his shoulders, his keen vision had locked onto his prey.

The young starling could see its predator but was either too immature or weak to take evasive action and it simply sat in a hunched position with its head back. It seemed to be waiting for some divine presence hopefully in the form of its mother landing beside it and rushing it out of danger, but its waiting seemed to be in vain for only the cat was to be seen as it slowly edged forward searching for the right spot to drop down into the garden out of sight of the young bird.

Samson heard the sound of the kitchen door open at the precise moment he sprang down, he crouched in the attack position when he heard the sound of the seven year old boy charge out into the garden.

Jamie had by this time forgotten the pain in his hand and also the birds presence as he tried to do hand stands on the lawn without much luck because his legs kept falling back, so he eventually gave up when he could not gain proper control of his legs.

Samson still had one eye on Jamie, as he crawled closer to the bird, on which he was preparing to pounce, when Jamie started kicking at an imaginary ball. Samson was not to be out done by the boy he had plenty of patience and would bide his time. At last the boy lost interest in his games and headed for the house. Samsons eyes followed Jamies departure from the garden, then his eyes returned to the helpless bird, now he could strike.

The starling let out a faint squeak which Jamies young ears picked up just as he was about to close the kitchen door, he turned towards the sound at the same moment as Samson sprang into action his whole body leaving the ground from the thrust of his back legs propelling it forward. Jamie screamed at the top of his voice, reaching higher notes than a soprano and charged towards the cat who, because of the sudden scream, had landed slightly to the side of the helpless bird his claws missing it.

`Go away, go away, go away.' screamed Jamie, Samson ran half way up the garden, stopped, and looked back at the boy who had cheated him by his shouting.

The bird stood in a petrified state as the boy dropped to his knees and closed his small hand firmly, but gently around the starling "Got - ya" he cried in delight.

The bird was silent as Jamie got to his feet, "I wonder where your mother is", said the boy looking up into the Hawthorne tree, "come on, me mam will give you something to eat".

The boy made for the kitchen door, and the cat who had jumped up on to the fence sat glaring at him and the prey that had got away.

"What have you got in your hand, oh, its a young bird", said his

41

mother as he walked into the kitchen, "don't let it out of your hand I'll see if I can find something to put it in". The boy's mother produced a shoe box, "here put it is this", the bird was gently lowered into the box by the boy.

The bird flapped its wings in a vain bid to clear the top of the box, but the boy placed his hand over the top barring its exit, and it gave up the struggle through exhaustion. It's beak wide open, the young bird sat waiting to be fed, the boys mother placed two of her fingers into a glass of water, then let the water drain from them, hoping some of the water would drop into the open beak, but she only had scant success.

The young bird would sooner have had its mother place a nice juicy worm into it's beak. While his mother tried to comfort the young bird, the boy had been in the garden pulling up hand fulls of grass for the bird to rest on, he placed the grass into the box, then looked up at his mother, "that will keep it warm", he said to his mother, "your quite right" she said.

"I know what we will do", she said to the boy, "we will wet some little pieces of bread and perhaps it will eat that", "do you think it will mum", "well we can try can't we" she continued.

However it was all in vain again, the young bird seemed unable to respond to the kindness from the boy and his mother.

The boy could see the concern on his mother's face for the bird, "do you think it will die mum", "no" she smiled "we will think of something", "I know lets put it in the tree, "mum, we can't do that, it will fall out then the cat will get it".

A sad look covered the boys countenance, "but it will die if we don't do something won't it"? She looked at him not sure what to say, yet her mind was searching for answers.

"I'm sure we will come up with the right idea", she continued, trying to comfort the seven year old, "I've got it mum, lets put the shoe box in the tree just like a nest, then the bird can't fall out", "now that's a good idea" she said.

So off they went into the garden, "here you hold the box and I will get the ladder out of the garden shed".

Jamie stood at the bottom of the garden watching his mother walking down with a small ladder, "this should get us up to the lower branches". While the ladder was placed in position Jamie spotted Samson sitting in the far corner of the garden, his eyes were not focused on Jamie but on the shoe box.

"Don't worry about him he won't be able to reach the bird when we put it up into the tree".

Jamie's mother stepped onto the ladder while Jamie passed the shoe box, the young bird was silent as it slid about in the box.

"Don't drop it mum, that Samson is still watching", his mother reached up into the tree to place the box between the trunk and a thick branch. When Jamie's mother was satisfied that she had the right balance for the shoe box, she looked into it to make sure the young bird was alright, and when she was satisfied she climbed down.

"Well that's it Jamie we can do no more". Jamie and his mum stood looking up into the tree and still sitting in the far corner was Samson who was also looking up into the tree. Jamie's mum walked back to the shed with the ladder, Jamie was following her but thought he would have one more look at the tree. "Mum, mum, look", she turned around to see the young bird's mother standing on top of the box with a big juicy worm in it's beak.

A typical Liverpool street scene c. 1930

45

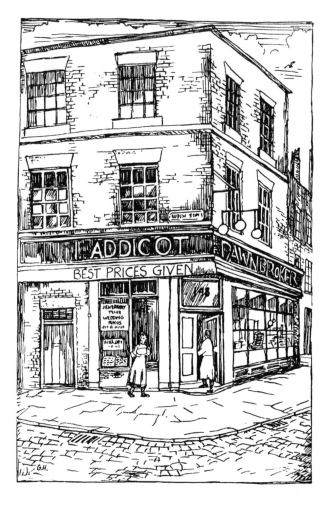

Addicot's Pawnshop made famous in the old Liverpool song
"Maggie Mae"

Addicott's Pawn Shop

Jamie Campbell was about five foot five with coal black hair, his eyebrows where very bushy. Two big bright blue eyes would hold you in their gaze when you looked into his face and the sides of his mouth would turn up and a smile would spread from ear to ear. He was slightly built yet his arms were covered in black hair, nature was wasting no time in turning him into a young man; just as well because he had entered the stage in his life early though it was when he would have to work for a living.

The cosy fireside and the Xmas tree adorned with presents and the counting of easter eggs each festive season, were never part of Jamie's young life but his parents had given him whatever they could afford to keep him healthy and strong.

The short walk from his house seemed to go on forever as he

thought about what lay ahead for him. Jamie was turning over in his mind what the man had said to him at the job interview.

"You must be clean and tidy and get here on time each morning, we start work at eight o'clock on the dot, so you must make sure you arrive here on time".

Jamie could see it was only twenty-to-eight by the clock fixed to the back wall of the pawn shop on the high street, its big round face looked out onto the street inviting people to look in through the shop window. Jamie's mother had made sure her son was well turned out to start his first job, he had an open neck check shirt with short sleeves and a navy blue v-necked pullover with no sleeves, the jacket that he used to wear for school was folded over his right arm because the sun was shining and it was too hot to wear. Jamie's grey pants were a bit shoddy and the creases had disappeared but they were clean, his shoes had a dullness about them because Jamie had spit on the shoe brush because there wasn't any black polish in the house.

Jamie looked at the big old house that had been turned into a pie factory the man at his interview told him that they make meat pies as well as other foodstuffs.

He was feeling a little nervous walking towards the side entrance door when he felt a heavy hand rest on his shoulder,` Come on lad or you will be late for work", Jamie looked up towards the voice and a big man with a big beaked nose looked down at him and ushered him through the doorway and into the pie factory.

As the rest of the work-force came into the building some of them greeted him while others just looked and ignored him.

Jamie had never seen so much food in his life, and at lunchtime he was given a plate of dinner by the lady who made the pies, so he did not have to eat the brawn sandwiches, covered in brown sauce that his mother had prepared for him.

Jamie's first day earning a living seemed to go on for ever, there was no big clock to look at like the one in Addicott's Pawn Shop but, the day went well for him, he felt comfortable in a nervous sort of way, the people who were showing him his duties were pleasant, but he yearned for the working day to come to an end so he could rush home to tell his mam what his first working day was like seeing meat pies made and ham shanks being cooked.

At last the long working day came to a close, he climbed the steps from the basement, leaving the ham shanks and meat pies made that day ready to go out in the van in the morning.

While Jamie stood with the other people waiting to put his card into the Time Clock Machine that would officially bring his first working day to a close, he noticed the man with the big beaked nose, standing in line with the rest of the work force, waiting for the clock to strike five, he had no jacket on and his shirt sleeves were turned up and he kept flexing the muscles in this forearms, most people didn't take notice of him, but Jamie smiled as he thought the beaked nose man looked a lot like Pop-Eye.

The next morning the sun was still shining as Jamie made his way to work feeling not quite so nervous about the Pie Factory, he looked into Addicott's Pawn Shop window and the clock was showing twenty-to-eight.

Jamie Campbell was always interested by the women he saw waiting outside of Addicott's on a Monday morning, some of them were old and had bundles of bedding balanced on their heads, and some were younger with children they all seemed to be trying to hold on to the kids with one hand and balance the bundle on their heads with the other.

But his young mind never wondered as to what would be on their beds for the rest of the week, but he did know what happened when his mother went to the Pawn Shop on a Monday morning with his dad's new shoes.

His dad would have to wear his working boots all week, but he never minded his shoes being in Addicott's just so long as the neighbours never knew that they had been taken there.

Sometimes Jamie's mother would forget to redeem the pledge on Saturday morning, which always resulted in his dad howling the house down, how could he go into the lounge bar on a Saturday night and parade himself, he would have to confine himself to the common bar instead.

Jamie moved on before he got too engrossed in the dealings that went on at Addicott's Pawn Shop.

The entrance to the Pie Factory was in sight when Jamie spotted ``beak nose", and he saw the momentum of his pace quicken as he tried to reach the doorway before two women, he was making sure that he was not going to be one of the last people to put his card in the time clock.

_Jamie was settling into his work at the Pie Factory. Most of his working day was spent cleaning and tidying up but he was getting to know more each day about the production of meat pies and boiled ham, the smell would make him feel hungry, and if the cook was in a good mood she would give him a hot cooked pie for his dinner.

The work was pleasant but Jamie never intended to stay for ever working in the cellar of the big old house making meat pies, he wanted to be able to see and mix with people in his working life and not be stuck in a cellar where the only people he would see would be the cook and a couple of other people and ``beak nose" when he came down to collect the pies and ham and other goodies to put in his van for delivering.

One of the things that broke up the monotony of the day was the appearance of the two bull terriers who made their way down into the basement from the offices on the top floor. The dogs would come down without the consent of their master who was one of the bosses. They were two friendly dogs, but Jamie thought they were slow and cumbersome, but he liked giving them titbits to eat, much against the cooks wishes, she warned him that he would be in trouble for encouraging the dogs, and, he could even get the sack for feeding them.

The bosses were always telling people off for feeding them, but Jamie never paid much heed to what the cook was trying to tell him, what's wrong with wanting to give a dog bits of food. Jamie himself would have loved to have a dog, but there wouldn't have been room in his little terraced home with his mam, dad, and the rest of the kids.

The Mullens next door to Jamie had a big dog but it had to sleep in the back yard in a wooden box with a tarpaulin sheet over it.

Jamie had hoped that his mother would let him to build a dog kennel in the back yard but she always said "I've already got a howling dog in the house – your father, the whole neighbourhood can hear him when I fail to collect his shoes from Addicott's on a Saturday morning".

Different members of staff would take the two dogs for a walk each day when they had finished their duties, but most days it would be ``beak nose" who, after completing his deliveries with the van, would rush in to take the dogs for a walk.

Jamie hoped that one day he may be asked to take one of the dogs for a walk in the park at the top of the road, and, in time his hopes were fulfilled. One day he had finished cleaning the floors in the cellar, the tables were spotless ready for the piemaking the next morning, when in walked ``beak nose," who asked the cook if Jamie could go with him to walk the two dogs.

It was like music to his ears when the cook said alright and he lost no time in getting his coat. The warm air and the rays of the sun greeted him as he emerged from the cool cellar at three o'clock on a beautiful mid-August day, it had been an exceptionally warm summer which had extended over until August.

The two dogs seemed pleased and they were so used to being taken for a walk by members of staff, that they sat, patient and waiting, but obviously eager to be moving, and as soon ``beak nose'' fastened the leads on the collars of the bull terriers, they were dancing around as dogs do when they feel happy, their short legs stamping the warm tarmac on the driveway.

"Here you take this one", said ``beak nose'' to Jamie "and don't go walking too fast, this sort of dog can't breath very well", he said. "Why don't they breath well", enquired Jamie. "I'm not sure, its something to do with their noses being flat". "Oh, I know what you mean, there's a fella in our street who's got a flat nose because he is always fighting and he is forever sniffing, just like them dogs with their podgy noses", continued Jamie. "That's enough talk said ``beak nose'' lets be getting on with it.

Jamie looked at ``beak nose'' who was walking a couple of paces in front of him, and he felt a sense of guilt come over him because he saw the man, not as a nice person, and somehow the name of ``beak nose'' had become implanted in Jamie's mind, and yet this is the same man who asked that Jamie be allowed to go and walk the dogs with him. Jamie was sure that they were going to the park at the top of the road, but ``beak nose'' seemed to have other plans as they walked along the busy main road.

The two dogs kept a steady slowish pace, their short legs kept putting the brakes on Jamie and his companion so a slow leisurely gait was the order of the day.

``Beak nose'' who was a few paces in front walked past the park entrance, with Jamie following, but on passing the two dogs gave a sideways glance at the entrance, their pace slowing and the lead dog found his neck being pulled forward as ``beak nose'' gave a slight pull on the lead to let it know he was not going into the park that day.

The sun was full in a cloudless blue sky and was moving towards them on its journey beyond the Wirral peninsula, and the heat of the day was not diminishing because no breeze could be felt.

Jamie and the two dogs had no say in the route ``beak nose'' was taking. Jamie felt that they were going in the wrong direction, but would not dare ask where ``beak nose'' was headed with the two dogs.

Taking the two dogs for a walk with ``beak nose'' was one thing but, the fourteen year old Jamie felt he had nothing in common with this man to be able to strike up a sort of dialogue with him, so like the two dogs Jamie was being lead by the collar to wherever it was that ``beak nose'' was headed.

Jamie could feel the warmth of the pavement through the thin soles of his shoes, and wonderd how the dogs must feel, with their paws in contact with the pavement. Jamie could hear them breathing heavily through their podgy noses and he felt sorry for them, and he could also see that ``beak nose'' was not at all concerned with the welfare of the dogs as their pace slackened as the walk progressed in the hot sun.

They eventually came to a halt as ``beak nose'' stopped to talk to a man who stepped out of a shop doorway. ``beak nose'' and the man kept a discreet distance from Jamie, and the two dogs where laying on their stomachs, their front paws pushed forward and their breathing still heavy, the older of the two dogs seemed to be gasping for breath.

Jamie and the dogs kept a silent posture except for the heavy breathing of the dogs while the two men continued to talk, eventually ``beak nose'' turned to Jamie with his hand stretched out, and pressed the lead of the other dog into Jamies hand, the dog looked up at ``beak nose'' as the lead was exchanged. Jamie was now standing in charge of not one dog, but two dogs.

`Take them back to the factory I wont be going back, I have some business too attend to you will be alright just take your time. 'Said ``beak nose'' then he turned and walked away with the other man, leaving Jamie on his own in charge of the two dogs.

Jamie gently pulled the two leads and the dogs slowy if somewhat reluctantly got to their feet. The older of the two dogs was having more difficulty walking, and the further they walked to get back to the factory, the pace was becoming slower, and Jamie was becoming anxious, and was hoping somebody from the factory would pass by to give him a hand, but help was not forthcoming.

The senior of the two dogs could go no further, his breathing was so bad that he collapsed in the doorway of the Salvation Citadel. Jamie could see that it was going to be immpossible to get the dog to its feet, the younger of the two dogs edged forward and pushed his nose into his fallen friends face but there was no response from his friend. The long walk and the heat of the day had taken its toll, and the heavy breathing ceased.

Jamie panicked and tried to get help from people passing by, but his pleas went unaided. People pretended not to notice his anguish, but at last a young boy who was younger than Jamie agreed to stand guard over the dog while Jamie made his way back to the factory with the other dog. At last he arrived back with the surviving dog in a very weak condition. Jamie was praying to himself that the dog would live, but he knew that he was in trouble because of ``beak nose''. The dog was carried upstairs to the office by one of the men in the factory.

The boss almost fainted when he saw his prize dog, and the women in the office were all crying and giving Jamie dirty looks, as though it was his fault for what had happened, then the questioning started and more dirty looks, eventually Jamie was told to go home and they would deal with him in the morning.

The big clock in Addicott's pawnshop had just chimed, seven thirty, Jamie stood looking into the window hoping that it would swallow him up, his young mind was confused and he kept starring at the clock, and feelling afraid of going to work at the pie factory, and at the same time not wanting to be late, the clock came up to, seven, forty five, and Jamie with a heavy heart made his way to the factory, it was no longer a joy to walk in the door and smell the freshly cooked meats, he felt only fear, and was afraid of what was to meet him when he entered the door.

Jamie knew he had done no harm to the dogs. ``beak nose" had left him to care for them on his own, but did the bosses know the truth about of what really happened, would they realise that he was also the victim just likc thc dogs, Jamie was not sure, and his feet wanted to turn around and walk the other way.

At last he was at his place of work and he was sure everybody was talking about him. `You have got your self in a right mess said the cook' `Yes but I'.......`Never mind telling me, it's the bosses you will have to explain to continued the cook. `I told them what happened last night, it was not my fault the dog died, ``beak nose", I mean the van driver, told me to bring them back on my own' protested Jamie. `Yes but you have more explaining about the dogs when the bosses see you.' `What do you mean cook.' Asked Jamie puzzled by the remark.' `never mind I'm saying no more.' said the cook.

Jamie felt very much on his own in the factory, the cook was a kind woman, but she had Jamie very worried by her remarks, and the rest of the workforce were no better for they just smiled at Jamie every time they passed him making his anguish much harder to bear. ``Beak nose" kept his distance loading the van with goods to deliver. And when ``beak nose'' had finished loading he was still hanging around the yard when he should have been out delivering and Jamie felt he looked like a worried man.

At last the waiting was over, a member of staff was sent to take Jamie up to the office. On his way he could see ``beak nose'' making his way up the stairs ahead of him, ``beak nose'' must have heard Jamie behind him on the stairs, but he never looked back, not even when he got to the bosses office. ``beak nose'' knocked on the door just as Jamie got to the top step

Jamie was told to wait until he was called into the office, he could here voices coming from within the voices got louder and ``beak nose'' could be heard above the rest of the people in the office. Little Jamies nerves sent him into a state of panic, but at last the long waiting was over, ``beak nose'' came running out of the office slammed the door behind him and made for the stairs without so much as a glance at Jamie, and attacked the stairs, in his descent like a wild goat in flight.

A woman came out of the office and invited Jamie in and standing behind the desk was the boss who towered above Jamie, also in the office where two more women standing by the window, the ladies were in full flow there were tears running down their cheeks, and the coloured handkerchiefs that patted the faces of the ladies could not hold back the tide that flowed from their eyes, and a sob was to be heard as they made eye contact with the bewildered Jamie.

Do realise that the two dogs have died, have you been mating the dogs is that the reason you took them yesterday, so tell me lad have you been mating them.' I don't know what you mean by mating them sir ?' `Did they have sex with other dogs.' The starkness of the reply from the boss brought about a flutter of the handkerchiefs and more sobs from the ladies `We will get to the truth of the matter because we are going to have an autopsy on the dogs and if the findings are not in your favour I will call the police in, do you understand.' `Yeah sir' replied Jamie, not understanding most of what the boss had been saying to him. `You and the van driver were the last two people to be seen with the two dogs, so I have no option but to dismiss you. The wages due to you can be collected when you finish work today.' Jamie could not believe what he had just heard, he looked in the direction of the sniffing ladies but they turned there backs on him to look out of the window.

Jamie felt humiliated having to work the rest of the day with people who only knew half of what had happened to the dogs, and ``beak nose" was nowhere to be seen, the one person who could confirm that Jamie was innocent of any wrong doing. The had stormed out of the building after his dismissal.

By the end of Jamie's last working day most people has ceased to make comment on the misfortune of the dogs and his dismissal.

When Jamie walked away from the Pie Factory for the last time, the bright sunny day had given way to dark clouds and blustery rain, making his plight that much harder to bear, but by the time he reached Addicott's Pawn Shop, the fourteen year old had already put the cruel events of the last few days behind him.

Jamie only glanced in the Pawn Shop window as he passed and he wondered whether his mother would be able to afford to get his dad's new shoes out of pawn at the weekend now that less money would be coming into the house, and he was unable to make a contribution to the domestic purse.

Jamie's father was sitting in front of the fire when he walked in and his mother was in the kitchen the smell of frying sausages permeated the small living room.

"How did you get on today" his mother shouted to him from the tiny kitchen. "I got the sack" "Oh my God" his mother cried, "The two dogs are dead", "Well you never killed the bloody dogs did you, so why did they sack you, it's that bloody van driver who caused it" said his mother as she left the frying sausages to walk into the living room, she looked at Jamie's father sitting by the fireside with the evening paper draped across his lap. "It's terrible" she said "I'm going around to see then over this" said his dad. He lifted one of his boots from the side of the chair.

"Just you stay where you are, things are bad enough for the lad without you making things worse" she cried at him. "Well the dogs could not have been very healthy if they snuffed it just because the sun was shining" he protested placing the boot back to the side of the chair.

Jamie sat down and waited for his mother to bring him a plate of sausage and egg, his mind was already filled with his future plans, and hoping he would find work very soon.

Jamie being the likeable lad that he was did not have to wait very long for another job of work to come his way. The man who owned Addicott's Pawn Shop had observed Jamie looking in the window on his way to the Pie Factory, and many is the time he had seen him with his mother in the shop, waiting to pawn her husband's good shoes, or any other item that would bring in a few shillings until the weekend.

Jamie was enjoying his new job and he didn't mind too much swapping the sweet smell of the pork pies and cooked ham shanks for the smell of bundles of bedding and sweaty shoes that he had to stow away onto the shelves in the back room of the Pawn Shop. His strong arms had no difficulty lifting the heavy bundles onto the shelves. At last he was meeting people while he was learning his new trade of Pawn Broker. The weeks went by and had given way to autumn and winter and he was given the chance to attend to the customers at the counter.

The painful memory of the dirty trick that ``beak nose" played on him by not telling the truth had faded into the recesses of his young mind.

Jamie felt quite smug as he looked out of the shop window, the big clock on the wall ticked away at the back of him, the ticking seemed so much louder because the shop was empty of customers and the only sounds came from the Pawn Shop keeper's heavy ledgers being turned over as he did his book-keeping during the quite spell.

Jamie could see the street outside was quiet because of the cold biting wind and he was so pre-occupied with what he could see from the window, that he failed to see a customer walking into the shop. "Jamie serve the man" came the stern voice of his employer. Jamic looked up to see a gents suite draped over the high counter and a pair of new shoes being placed on the top of the suite. "How much can I have for those", Jamie looked up to the sound of the familiar voice, only to find himself starring into the eyes of ``beak nose". "I'll give you, five shillings, take it or leave it" said Jamie without waiting for his employers assessment..

Jamie stood and watched closely as ``beak nose" started to protest at the small amount offered but Jamie repeated take it or leave it and ``beak nose" growled alright if that's the best you can do I'll take it.

We'll make a Pawn Broker of you yet said Jamies boss go and put the kettle on there's a good lad Jamie glanced out of the window in time to see ``beak nose" cross the road pulling the collar of his jacket around his ears and clutching his five shillings.

Collecting street rubbish Liverpool center c. 1900

The Mourners

We where all seated on the hard backed chairs, the backs of which were pushed back to the walls in the front parlour room of the old Victorian House.

All the available space around the walls of the room had a chair in it, and, each chair was occuppied by a mourner, all seemed to be competing with the large oak sideboard with triple framed mirrors. The floral patterned wall paper was turning to a sickly yellow colour in the places where it came into contact with what the rays of sun that managed to penetrate the curtains in the bay window.

Some of the mourners looked at the floor, others looked nervous as they tried sometimes without much success to find a comfortable resting place for their posteriors' on the straight backed wooden chairs.

The mourners had been gathered by the sudden death of Tommy Murphy. Most of the people in the room were still in a state of shock from learning of the sudden departure of Tommy. No one expected him to take his leave so soon, I mean to say, he was only fifty nine year old, and to those getting on in years he was still a young man, and to those who were younger he still didn't seem to be that old, but still he was going to be missed by old and young alike.

The room for the mourners was provided by Tommy's landlady. She was a good soul who had looked after Tommy since his divorce after only two years of marriage and was like a second mother to him putting up with his moods of depression each time his money ran out and his trouser pockets contained only the stale odour from his perspirations.

Most of what Tommy earned would be handed over the bar counter at his local Pub. He would buy friend or stranger whatever alcoholic refreshment they were attracted to.

Most of the mourners were unknown to one another, relations, friends and distant relatives, some had attended out of respect and some to save face. Tommy would have introduced all of them had he still been in a position to do so but being laid out in the local chapel of rest made that task impossible even for him.

Standing on the doorstep of the terraced house were two of Tommy's friends it was their job to keep a look out for the hearse making its way to the house from the chapel of rest. One of the men a tall thin fellow with reddish cheeks and a nose to match was wearing a dark suite that had seen better days and was not meant for his height, the tall man had his hands in his trouser pockets trying to push the bottom of the trouser leg downwards in the hope that it would make contact with the top of his shoes. The second man stood to the side of the doorway with his back to the wall he was a short stocky man smoking a cheroot, every time he had a drag at the cigar the smoke covered his pale round face, his belly protruded over the top of his dark grey trousers which had been bought special to enable him to create a good impression at the funeral, and his dark leather jacket gave him an air of authority every time he pulled his belly in and took another drag at his cheroot.

An elderly aunt of Tommy's was quietly sitting by the oak sideboard and thinking about the Mass card that she had for her nephew in the vain hope it may assist in speeding his ascent into heaven. It would have been nice, she thought, if he could have been laying in an open coffin in the empty space in the middle of the room with everybody sitting around paying there last respects, but then she wondered if he would ever get to heaven, him being a terrible drinker and womaniser.

She was glad his mother was not here at such a sad time as she would not have been very happy knowing that Tommy would not be going to a plot in the cemetery to rest along side her and his father. "God have mercy on them", the elderly aunt muttered to herself, "poor Tommy will just be a tin of ashes leaving the crematorium".

Tommy liked his beer but then life had offered him precious little else, he was a kind and humble man who asked little from life, and little is what he got, God gave him a six foot frame, blue eyes and a stammer. That's what Tommy would tell his friends during one of his blue moods, but he had the sort of personality that had won him many friends.

Any money that Tommy earned from his labours as a seaman, soon slipped through his fingers, money was not for saving it was meant to derive pleasure, and most of Tommy's fulfilment came from standing in the bar of his local Pub declaring Murphy's back in town. He would bang his two fists on the bar, then like the 'town crier inform everyone of the assembled drinkers, whether they be friend or foe that the drinks were on him.

The merry making would go on all day and night until closing time. The following morning Tommy would be lucky to have the price of a pint in his pockets. When the chips were down and Tommy's pockets empty he would be hoping that one of his many friends would rescue him from the depths of despair by their generosity.

And now that he had gone, his friends had come to pay their last respects, but not only that, they also made the arrangements for his funeral. Tommy had made many friends, far more that even he realised, God gave him a stammer but he also gave him the ability to communicate with his personality and sense of fairness. He was the sort of man that would take a hungry stray dog home with him to feed it.

In the last few months of Tommy's life he had started to save some of the money that he had earned from his labours, the money was to be used for the only holiday he would have had in his life time, but it was not to be, for fate had already mapped out the final chapter in his life. But before his sudden departure he had given instructions that the small amount in his post office savings book should be used to celebrate his departure.

The tall man with the uncomfortable suite turned and poked his head into the lobby, "there here, there on the way down the road", his voice gaining a higher pitch, "I see the hearse".

The mourners inside started to move into the lobby led by Tommy's elderly aunt, "he was a good man, never did anybody any harm" she kept muttering to herself.

Still at the front door the man with the leather jacket, the last of the cheroot between his fingers, marching the mourners to the two funeral cars behind the hearse, the elderly aunt climbing into the front car, turned to the woman behind her, "you know I shouldn't be in the first car I hardly ever saw poor Tommy" the woman just smiled the way people do at a funeral and guided the old lady into the car.

The hearse pulled away from the house followed by the mourners cars, but in close pursuit where about fifteen private cars carrying Tommy's friends from his local Pub.

A lone piper was waiting to lead the coffin into the church, followed by the relations who only turn up when ever there is a funeral. The people inside filled every pew and throughout the church and into the street could be heard the strains of 'The lark in the clear air' then the pipes fell silent for the mass to begin, the priest spoke of the man as he had known him all his life, and he was impressed by the man who had gone to sleep forever, he talked about the dear departed soul who left no wealthy positions or works of art, yet he could attract so many people at his parting.

The pipes fell silent after the last lament and Tommy laid to rest.

"He could have still been with us if only he had been a good boy", cried Tommy's aunt as she climbed into the car for the ride back to the house with the rest of the mourners.

Most of Tommy's friends headed for the local Pub to carry out Tommy's last wish, to celebrate his leaving.

The beer flowed and the laughter rose, no mood of remorse could be felt, the thoughts and the talk was of Tommy and other old friends who had passed on. Some one remarked after nine, or was it ten pints that he was sure that he could hear the sound of two fists pounding the bar and bellowing,

` Murphy's back in town'.

Typical childrens playground Liverpool c. 1930

7

Black Jack's

It was always referred to as 'Black Jacks" it was one of many Pubs in the area, when local people decided to have a few jars it would be in 'Black Jacks', that was the name of our local and that name remained for the premises throughout my childhood.

It was only later in my life that I took the trouble to read the large gold painted letters, 'The Clyde Public House' above the frosted glass window, and realised its true name.

Like most children I took more notice of the spoken word, so Black Jacks became imprinted in my mind, but it was after discovering the correct name that I decided to find out the true nature of the name Black Jack, so I decided to ask my dad thinking he would be the one to give me the right answers.

"Well its like this", he said, "Many years ago the Manager was a big fella with a back as straight as a guardsman, and he was from County Kerry", and, although I nodded in agreement I did not have any inkling of where or what County Kerry was.

"He had a head of hair as black as coal, just like your mother, he had a black beard that seemed to cover most of his face, and although a gentle giant of a man, he was still a fearsome sight especially if any one decided to disturb the peace in his establishment. He was always referred to as Black Jack, so that's how the name came about".

"Is he still in the pub" I required, "no he is long since gone and I imagine he will be up there with the angels".

Black Jacks backed onto the Leeds and Liverpool Canal, where most of the lads in the area had their first swimming lessons, but I don't remember any of the girls in the area taking the plunge, but then who could blame them, they must have had more sense than to jump into a canal that was often used as a common dumping ground.

A dead dog or cat floating by never got in the way of your enjoyment, and, as we never had the luxury of going to the swimming baths with a towel, a pair of swimming trunks and the entrance fee, we had to leave it to mother nature to provide for us.

When the swimming session was over we would stand shivering on the bank with our hands crossed waiting to share the one towel between six or seven lads that's if we were lucky of course. .

Many a drama was played out in that canal; most times they would be happy but on other occasions they could be sad, the canal was no respecter of persons.

The Leeds and Liverpool Canal twisted and turned its way down to the River Mersey and Black Jacks continued to offer liquid refreshments and the chance to relax from the rigours of life.

I suppose to most people in this enlightened age it would seem like a strange Hostelry, but it served its purpose, it was only a very small establishment and the bar was adorned by men only, not that women weren't allowed in it, but no self respecting women would want to stand with men packed in like sardines in a tin. They would stand shoulder to shoulder when it was busy, but it did not matter if there was a little inconvenience every body knew one another.

But if a man was to take his wife into Black Jacks he would take her into the parlour and he would stride along the street with his head held high like a soldier on parade and the only movement of his head would be to glance down at his shining shoes.

After ordering a pint for himself and a half pint for his missus they would each take a sip just to get the taste buds active, then silence would cloud their thoughts, they would sit and stare ahead without so much as a word spoken to one another.

So this was the start of a night out together, and the silence would only be broken when he decided to lift the pint glass from the table and put it to his lips, followed closely by his wife with her half pint of Guinness the creamy head still on it, their lips would move in unison and their glasses would return to the table at precisely the same time.

The pattern was exactly the same for the other couples in the parlour except for just the odd couple who had something to talk about due to the fact that they were courting all the other residents in the parlour trying not to look at them by staring straight ahead or looking down at the floor, but in reality every body was listening intensely to every word that the courting couple uttered.

Around about 9 or 9.30 their cheeks would start to flush which was a sign that the tensions of life was gradually lifting from their shoulders. The 'gargle' would flow more freely bringing an end to the formal silence, the chat would now become spontaneous and the songs would start, those with passable voices would be asked to sing again.

The parlour would now be full, not a seat empty, and the beer on the bar counter would be covered in nicotine if it had not been consumed within a few minutes, but the delight of Black Jacks, were the group of lovely old ladies who sat on wooden forms along the passage way of the Pub. The passage way started at one door and went round at a forty-five degree angle to the next door, because the pub was on the corner of the street and the wooden forms followed it around.

The old ladies where the last of an age that was even then speedily moving on, they sat like clucking hens clutching their glasses of stout, most of them sat with shawls around their shoulders to keep out the draught from the doors at either end of the passage way, and I can never remember them wearing anything else other than long dark skirts, and never an ankle on view. This I suppose also helped to keep out the chill wind that made its way along the passage every time somebody tried to gain entrance.

The ladies would sit on the long wooden forms without a speck of comfort but would be happy talking amongst themselves, and paying little heed to what went on either in the parlour at the back of them nor the bar filled with men uttering some of the most vile obscenities especially if it was on a Saturday night, when most of them had strong opinions as to the state of the local football results.

The ladies sitting in the passage would never be lost for words and would constantly break into hilarious laughter. They would offer a pinch of snuff to one of the men from the bar who was making his way to the toilet.

Most of them seemed to take snuff and would keep it in a small tin with a removable lid, or if they had a son or husband who went away to sea, they could be in possession of a nice coloured snuff box that had been brought home for them; for women, smoking was frowned upon in public in that day and age.

Most of the old ladies had never had a holiday in their lives and hardly moved more than a mile or so out of the area where they lived and life was very harsh for them, they had few material possessions, but they did have a lot of dignity and strength of character. To sit in Black Jacks for a couple of hours once or twice a week was the reward for a life time of hard work.

They had neither the time to have a nervous break-down or the money or visit the doctor except in absolute dire emergencies bordering on death, most cures for their ailments had been passed down to them from parents who had been born long before the nineteenth century came to a close.

Their shawls always seemed to be well made and heavy to keep at bay the cold and damp of the winter days. The better shawls had shapely tassels hanging from them and the women's hair was always tied at the back in a bun shape.

Those stout hearted dignified women sitting in a row along the passage way had given birth to a generation, whose hopes for the future would in the main, be counted by the material things in life, but they expected only the bare necessities to keep them alive.

They helped to make the future yet they were from the past they had come from the nineteenth century with the values of their youth into a rapidly changing twentieth century, witnessing two world wars, but the changing new world had not really affected or changed them.

Boris

He was a big fella, and very proud, — you could tell that by the way he walked, — his back straight, you could say, rigid, his head held high but it did nothing to impair the agility in his walk,.

Boris had a white coat with a touch of red around his head which came down to encircle his right eye. His tail was mostly red with a few streaks of white. The tail was long and bushy and stood up like a skunk, but came down in a straight line with his body when ever he was stalking his prey which could be anything from a bird to a mouse.

Boris was good at fending for himself. Tins of cat food were never on his menu when he was master of the back yard walls such luxury was unheard of in his neck of the woods; — well back entries to be precise. Boris had never paid a visit to the vet to patch up any of his war wounds, nature was his vet, he just got on with life, with the exception of the time he broke his leg. Boris like most felines was definately his own master, but he also had to have a nice cosy fireside to come home too, especially after he had been out on a cold winters night. On entering the house he would run his head and body across the legs of the first person he encountered, making sure of a warm welcome for him.

One morning after a night on the tiles it was clear to everybody that his front right leg was broken. Everyone in the household was concerned running around not sure what to do, but eventually two flat pieces of wood were produced, a narrow bandage and a roll of plaster tape. Two pair of hands held Boris down whilst the third person pulled his broken leg back into position, then the crude operation was completed by placing a flat piece of wood on each side of his leg then the bandage and plaster tape wrapped tightly around the crippled leg making sure Boris would not be able to pull it away.

Most of Boris's wounds were of a minor nature, but this one would keep him confined to the house for some time until the pain had subsided.

Living in the same household was a large dog who was the same colour as Boris, mostly white but with a coat that turned black when it got to the right side of his face giving one white ear and the other black. Boris never took much notice of him although he was not a bad dog well, he was good to Boris, he would look after him when they were out in the street together, no other dog would go near Boris when his canine friend was about. Not that Boris could not take care of himself, he was more than able for most predators that came his way.

One source of enjoyment for Boris was trotting alongside his friend when he was on the lead out for a walk with his master, Boris being almost the same colour as his friend, would cause a deal of amusement amongst the neighbours the tall dog with his long legs and Boris running alongside him. If Boris did have an enemy it was the German Sheperd dog that lived next door, he was a big handsome dog with a long coat of fur that hung from his sides, his colour was fawn with black streaks, and generally he was a good natured fellow, but his one weakness was that he did not like cats. He never liked Boris from the first time he could scale the back yard walls when he was little more than a kitten, I imagine there was a fair bit of jealously on the part of the German Shepherd because he was confined to the back yard and Boris was as free as a bird.

I suppose it must have been hard on him having to walk up and down, and around in circles all day in a small back yard bored out of his mind, then to see a kitten walking along the back yard wall able to stroll wherever he wanted to must have driven him nearly insane. His only freedom if you could call it that was to trot alongside of your master when he took you out on the lead.

Boris like all kittens was very playful and when he discovered that he could scale the walls for the first time would stroll along the top of the wall goading the poor dog whilst getting to know the neighbourhood he would look the dog straight in the eyes, until the dog turned his back on Boris, breaking eye contact.

Boris was becoming king of the back yard walls and, as the months went by, he had the pick of the female cats, as he was growing into a big handsome fellow, but his handsome looks gave cause for a lot of bickering amongst the neighbourhood Tom cats, so Boris was frequently attacked, but he was a match for any Tom who tried to encroach onto his territory.

As the months went by Boris got stronger, and the German Shepherd became more frustrated watching the cat upon the wall enjoying life everyday, pleasing himself what he did, but perhaps the worst part was having to put up with Boris starring down at him everyday, so the German Shepherd started to bark at Boris but the barking had little or no effect on Boris he would still continue to stare down at the dog, and he seemed to get great satisfaction from the poor dog becoming agitated by the constant eye contact.

During the summer months when the sun was shining, Boris had taken to lounging on the back walls, sometimes his tail hanging down into the yard next door, it was one of those days when Boris had been giving the dog one of his starrings. Boris had sat down to enjoy the warm rays of the sun, his tail flicking up and down every time the flies, which always seemed to appear on warm days, had landed on his back, every time the flicking of the tail stopped, it would hang down against the back wall, Boris started to dose off, unaware that the German Shepherd was watching the flicking tail, the dog slowly got to his feet from sitting position and made his way towards the wall this his tormentor was sleeping on.

The shepherd dog stood to his full height while looking up at the limp tail, and he never took his eyes from it as he went into a crouching position, his front legs pushing his weight against his back legs, when he had worked out the exact distance between himself and the tail he gave one mighty push and sprung into action, he went up to wall like a pole vaulter, his strong jaws tightened around the tip of Boris's tail, the dog fell back onto his hind legs with a look of satisfaction in his eyes as he looked up at Boris, who was making a terrible screeching sound as he looked down into the eyes of his attacker.

The days and weeks went by and Boris's tail healed up, but he never forgot what the German Shepherd had done to him. Boris still continued to goad the dog by standing on the wall and starring down at him, but everytime Boris annoyed the dog, he would jump up the wall hoping to get to grips with his tormentor once again. But it was not to be, it was Boris who was on the offensive, waiting for the right time when he could strike back. Boris was back to his tricks again, walking up and down the wall, with the dog jumping up still trying to make contact. Boris pushed his nose down towards the leaping dog, his face being pushed further down without losing balance.

Boris waited while the dog came even closer each time he leaped up the wall. Boris knew he had to get his timing right, the German Shepherd leaped into action, his jaws open as he came out to meet Boris, but Boris struck first his claw fully extended as it made contact like a cutlass, slicing through the tip of the dogs nose, the dog was yelling and howling as it ran around the yard. The weeks passed as the two combatants kept to their own territory, but in the course of time Boris eventually made his way down into the yard and sat along side his old enemy.

Liverpool working wife c. 1900

The Weaker Sex

Ausey's emotions ran high as he looked into the battered but quite clear photograph that a friend had just discovered, he looked into the many faces, some he recognised from his childhood, their eyes stared back at him frozen in time, about 40 women, and ten men.

He looked at the faces, trying hard to put a name to each of them, some names came easy, but others took a little more time. Many of the names of the people who were looking out at him had receded into the depths of his mind, but they all seemed to be willing him to remember them. The task was a pleasant one and the names came forward slowly one after the other after more than a forty year span.

Between two large ladies sat Mrs. Dixie a diminutive figure

with a smile that gave her cheeks a pleasant roundness, but the smile seemed strained. It could have been because of her having just finishing the strenuous task of pushing a hand cart through the streets of Liverpool selling fruit and vegetables but, whatever the cause, it had taken much effort, that was certain.

Mrs. Dixie was one of the (so called) weaker sex, but in reality she must of had the strength of a shire-horse. She sat posing a little embarrassed for the photograph before setting out on a mystery coach trip that was to take her and her neighbours out into the countryside for a few hours, relaxation in a country Pub away from the toil of feeding and caring for their families in their closely knit community.

Mrs. Dixie was much admired and respected by the community at large. She was out of her bed no later than five o'clock on six mornings each week, hail, rain or snow, this little lady who set a good example to the whole community. If you wanted to feed yourself and kids you had to be prepared to put up with the suffering. When you are young you can not be expected to see or understand the pain that women like Mrs. Dixie had to contend with every day of their lives.

When she was not engaged in pushing her hand-cart and selling her wares, people would be knocking on her door, in the hope that she would be able to get them a clothing ticket off Mr. Levy the Jewman, as he was affectionately known.

Mrs. Dixie was a collecting agent for Mr. Levy, and every Friday evening at six o'clock he would knock on the door, which was nearly always already open for him, "are you there, Mrs" he would shout, "Oh come in Mr. Levy", she would reply and he would walk into the kitchen where he would find Mrs. Dixie sitting at a highly scrubbed table which smelt strongly of carbolic soap.

She would be sitting there with an empty chair alongside her for Mr. Levy to sit on, small amounts of coinage would be stacked in little piles in front of her, and a few pound notes under the sugar basin, her little note book in front of her, with the stub of a pencil tucked inside of it.

After making himself comfortable, Mr. Levy always opened his order book in front of him and the scene was set for the weekly ritual of their little business venture.
"Well what have you got for me this week, Mrs".
"Everyone has paid, except Billy McGuire," she said, "could he pay three shillings next week, because he's had no work this week, and he's a good lad".
"I suppose if he hasn't any money we will just have to wait untill next week", said Mr. Levy.
"How right you are" said Mrs. Dixie.
"I've collected three pounds, nineteen shillings and sixpence".
Mr. Levy checked the amount, then turned to Mrs. Dixie with a smile and pushed the commission towards her. "You've done well this week",
Mrs. Dixie put her small commission into her purse.
 "Well now who wants what, this week, Mrs"
"Tommy Davies could do with a new pair of boots, he's just got a job on the docks", "right, so he wants boots, what size",

continued Mr. Levy who was writing on a small ticket to be given to Tommy Davies who would take it into town and exchange it at a clothing warehouse for a pair of boots.

"And can I have a ticket for Mrs. Conner's eldest lad, he's getting married in two weeks time to Mrs. Daly's youngest daughter". And while Mr. Levy was writing the details on the tickets for Mrs. Dixie's neighbours, Mrs. Dixie was pouring the boiling water into the large teapot on the table next to her, this was left to brew on the brass hob in front of the coal fire at her back, when the required time had elapsed she reached for the big brown tea-pot and poured a cup for herself and Mr. Levy. "Your stomach must be as tanned as the inside of this tea-pot, your just as bad as that man of mine with your strong tea" said Mrs Dixie.

"Well your drinking it Mrs", "only when I make it for you and that fella of mine" she replied.
"Anyway, this is the way it is with you women, if you weren't telling me and that man of yours off, you would be having a go at the poor cat", "indeed I would not" she said. Mr. Levy smiled, and got on with his work in between sipping his tea.

"Nobody touches that mug I keep it just for you" she said. "I know Mrs, you tell me every week you save it just for me". "Oh do I". Mrs. Dixie's cheeks flushed, and she moved uneasy on her chair.
"Anyway, its good of you to do that just for me", said a reassuring Mr. Levy.

"And while I think on, Mrs. McCarthy could do with a new suit for one of her boys', she lost her husband yesterday, and the lad hasn't a decent set of clothes for his father's funeral".

Mr. Levy looked up over the top of his specs, "how sad Mrs".

"How right you are Mr. Levy, and to think one day we will all go the same way, if God spares us".

Mr. Levy chose not to get involved any further in the subject and continued with his book work, and silence prevailed over the sparsely furnished room.

A hissing sound from the gas mantle above Mr. Levy's head disturbed the peaceful scene, and the light was deflected to fall like a veil about him on to the bare table.

Ausey could picture the scene, with Mrs. Dixie and Mr. Levy, being played out every Friday like a reoccurring theatrical performance. The banter from the two of them was imprinted and stored away in his mind, and the fond memories had been brought out of storage by the old photograph that beckoned him to look deep within.

"Well I'll be going Mrs" said Mr. Levy closing his order book, before putting the lose coinage into a small black bag made of shiny material. "Do you mind if I go down the yard first Mrs".

"Of course I don't, you should know that by now Mr. Levy".

He turned the handle of the rim-lock and walked out into the small back yard, to be guided by the faint glow from the gas-light that shone through the kitchen window on the yard, which gave him a chance to grope his way along the unlit wall, his hand reached out for the latch to the lavatory door.

Once inside he began feeling for the lavatory pan, in order to aim dead centre while relieving himself, then after fixing his attire, his hand swept across the width of the lavatory to engage the chain that hung from the high level system.

Returning from the yard, Mr. Levy gently closed the kitchen door, picked up his cash bag and the rest of the items used in his trade as a credit draper and bid Mrs Dixie good night.
"Good night Mr. Levy, good night and God bless".

Ausey had seen the stage setting of Mrs. Dixie and Mr. Levy being played out every Friday evening for many years, when he was a boy, He would always be on call to run errands for the hard working Mrs. Dixie, and he would sometime deliver the clothing tickets to some of the people who had requested them, but most of the time the neighbours would be shouting up the lobby of the little terraced house before Mr. Levy was half way up the street.

"Are you there Mrs. Dixie, can we come in", the long wait was over, they had emerged from behind their house curtains waiting for Mr. Levy to go on his way. Smiles would be on the faces of the womenfolk, clutching their clothing tickets after leaving the little terraced house.

Ausey looked back at the sea of faces that stared out at him, "God this photograph could tell a thousand stories", he shook his head as he looked back into the eyes of the women, his mind was full of guilt and admiration for them. He looked at them all in turn knowing that each of them had a story to tell in the struggle to survive, but they would be thankful for a trip by coach into the countryside for a few hours once or twice a year, organised by the very able Mrs. Mills, another one of the smiling women on the photograph before him.

The few hours spent in the country would always finish by relaxing in the local Pub. The fond memories of Mrs. Dixie and the rest of them will be imprinted on my mind forever, thought Ausey.

To think of stupid politicians prattling on about women maybe becoming the bread winners, a great pity yhat non of them had lived in the poorer parts of Liverpool then they would know what hard work was all about. Mrs. Dixie and her neighbours were all sentenced to hard labour the day they were born".

As Ausey tried to tear his gaze away from the women in the photograph, his imagination ran away with him and he saw in his minds eye Mrs. Dixie pushing her hand-cart, and the rest of the women waving to him as they followed Mrs. Dixie down the street.

The "Weaker Sex" going to the washhouse c. 1950

90

10

Smudge and the Twins

Smudge was a handsome dog he was a cross between an alsation and some other canine, who's identity was in grave doubt. Smudge was the size of a labrador, had the build of a cocker spaniel, and the speed of a greyhound.

Smudge's white coat and large black spots combined with his long legs, made him stand out from all the other mongrels in the area, he was also smart and cunning and was a favourite with the local kids, but he was not a favourite with people on push bikes or even those on motor bikes, he would chase anyone that dared to pass him.

Smudge was also a bit of a coward, he would take great pleasure in chasing any dog that was smaller than him, but when he encountered a dog on a lead this was his opportunity to show who was master, big or small it never mattered, they were for the taking. It had been known for Smudge to have a go at larger dogs than himself, to test their metal so to speak, if they backed down Smudge would show them who was superior, and after frightening the life out of them he would walk away proudly down the road with his head up.

If by chance the unsuspecting canine could defend him or herself, Smudge would sometimes take a beating which sent him skipping down the road with his tail between his legs, losing no time at all to gain the shelter of his home and his two companions Billy and Freddy.

Billy and Freddy were ten year old twins, tall for ten year olds they each had a mop of blonde hair, blue eyes, and healthy bodies.

Wherever the twins could be found Smudge was not too far away, the three of them were inseparable. Their playground was concentrated anywhere along the dock road and all streets running up from the docks, between the Gladstone Dock and the Pierhead on the Liverpool water front.

The twins ran free like the wind, and Smudge was always by their side. Billy and Freddy were two of five children, their father had died three years before. The mother of the twins could do little with them, they were very self assured, and would take little notice of their mother or anybody else for that matter, certainly not the teachers in school; the boys were not cheeky, but appeared to be single minded, staying away from school whenever the opportunity presented itself.

Smudge was never on a lead and never wore a collar, according to the twins, only pampered dogs had a collar and allowed themselves to be led about on a lead, that was one of their firm beliefs.

The two boys had a way with animals that no other kids in the area had, give them any animal you cared to choose and they could get it to perform some trick or other in a matter of minutes, but dogs were their favourite.

Although Smudge who was not much younger than the boys loved being with them but he did however have one weakness, he was in love with an alsation, not an ordinary one oh no, she was a police dog!

Whenever he saw her, he would become so gentle even to making himself look foolish. He would roll over on his back lying at her feet and making all sorts of daft noises. Smudge was so enchanted with her that he would forget about the twins, no amount of entreating would stop him from performing his peculiar courtship procedeure. The twins and the policeman would be totally ignored by both animals and left standing looking on and no amount of coaxing would drag Smudge from his lady love until his courtship display was over.

While Smudge was performing his ritual the policeman would

be laughing at him and the twins would be calling him such names as, "your stupid daft dog", "me mam said we should have drowned you at birth, "she's right you daft ticket".

It was only when the police dog got fed up with his courtship display, by turning her back on him and walking away and giving Smudge a backward glance, would he come to his senses and go skipping down the road to catch up with the twins who had always by then walked away and left him.

When Smudge caught up to the twins, Billy turned to Freddy, "Its your fault he is like this making a show of himself", "no its not" said an indignant Freddy, "He is in love and that's what happens when people or animals fall in love".

"But he is only a dog and me dad said they don't fall in love", said Billy determined to get the better of Freddy.

"I know he is only a dog but me mam said they can fall in love just like humans".

And so the argument went on until something else distracted their minds.

School work was not a priority with the twins so every chance they got to sag school they would do so, the thought of being punished would never deter them. There was a lot of adventures out on the streets and that's where they always like to be, running wild with Smudge, their faithful friend who sat outside the school no matter what the weather was like waiting for his two little friends to appear.

School holiday time was the time the twins liked best of all, it gave them the chance to go thieving without having to go to school the next day and thieving and robbing was what they had become good at, school work only got in the way of taking what was not theirs.

It wasn't as though the boys came from a dishonest family, their mother was a good woman with three younger children in addition to her extrovert ten year old twins. The boys father had died in tragic circumstances at work. After the death of their father the boys grew restless and wandered further away from home in their adventures with Smudge their constant companion.

Smudge was supposed to sleep in the lobby under the stairs but most nights the twins would sneak him up stairs to sleep at the bottom of their bed.

Every morning when the twins where getting ready for school, that's if they had chosen to go to school, instead of 'sagging', Smudge would be on the door step waiting to lead the way, but whether it was school or doing a 'bunk', Smudge would be out in front skipping along the road like a greyhound, Freddy and Billy would be looking all about them to see if there was an opportunity to take something which did not belong to them.

Taking what was not their's was part of the adventure of sagging school, it provided them with excitement, and it also gave them respect from their school friends, the chance to 'show-off' displaying what they had stolen. Most of what they had taken would be cast to one side, like throwing an old pair of boots in the bin, or they would swap for a bag of sweets from an older more cunning school friend.

The twins knew that they could get away with taking a bag of sweets home with them, but they would never get away with taking the proceeds of their day of adventure home with them.

The twins mother was well aware of the boys running wild so she was always on the look out to make sure they brought nothing into the house that did not belong to them.

Smudge was still leading the way, but stopping from time to time sniffing the scent of some other animal that had gone before him, and the boys at times would be hoping that the police dog did not appear, resulting in Smudge going into his daft repertoire so, if the twins saw the police dog first, they would call Smudge and dodge down a side street to get him away from her.

The boys liked nothing better than to walk along the dock road, sometimes casting an eye above the fence that encompassed the dock estate to see the masts and funnels of the ships using the port. But most of the time they would be looking into the warehouses and factories that ran the length of the road.

The twins had a plan of action, they had trained Smudge to walk in to a warehouse or any other establishment that may give easy pickings, the dog would distract people by his friendlessness, and it would give the boys a chance to look about and slip anything into their pockets that had taken their fancy.

Smudge was such a capable and intelligent dog that they had taught him to stand outside on the pavement and bark if anybody was passing the building that they had entered — a window that had not been securely fastened presented few problems to the agile twins.

On one occasion the twins had entered a building after closing time, leaving Smudge on guard duty outside, while the boys' were blundering their way through a warehouse full of boxes of oranges, apples, and all sorts of exotic fruits from abroad, they felt a sense of excitement and adventure in what they were doing, safe in the knowledge that Smudge was keeping watch outside.

Anything that the twins could stuff into their pullovers that had been pushed into their trousers went in, if they could not eat it, in it went until their pullovers had ballooned out and they could no longer carry anymore. They were like two pirates ripping open the fragile wooden boxes.

Smudge had not given a warning bark so they slipped out of the front door of the building and walked out onto the pavement, only to find Smudge laying on his back looking up into the eyes of the police dog and the policeman staring at their bulging pullovers.

You must admit that dog of yours is pretty foolish over my dog said the policeman but you two must be the prize idiots of all time to place your trust in him the way he is at the moment so your both nicked — get the picture do you? — well if you don't now you soon will when the magistrate starts on you, to say nothing about what your mother is going to do to you both.

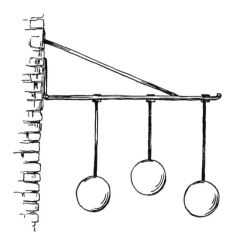

11

Confession

Brendon walked into the church with the guilt of a condemned man waiting to come face to face with his executioner and almost on tip toe he advanced towards the confessional box.

With his head half turned he could see two old ladies, a young man and a boy who went to the same school as himself. They were all waiting to have their confessions heard. Brendon sat down in the empty pew to await his turn.

Time seemed to stand still for Brendon as the people in front of him disappeared into the confessional box. He listened to the door click each time they went in, and listened for the gentle thud of the door lock every time they came out. Brendon looked at every one of them as they emerged and watched each one as they went and knelt down to do their act of contrition, asking for forgiveness for their sins. "Their sins could not be as big as mine", Brendon kept repeating to himself.

He waited for the thud of the confessional box door as the boy who went to his school came out. The sound though low pitched, reverberated around the almost empty church as Brendon pulled himself to his feet and walked towards the solid oak door that would lead him into the dimly lit cubical. He sat down beside the partition that separated him from his parish priest. He could see the outline of the priest's head and shoulders as he stared into the screen, then as dreadful fear gripped him the words came tumbling out:

"Bless me I have sinned", said Brendon, his eyes closed.

"Can we start again", and do it right this time" said the priest, ""Bless me father for I have sinned".

"That's better, now lets go on" said the priest, sensing Brendon's state of mind. "I used swear words seven times this week — I was cheeky to my mam — I kicked next door's cat because it was crying on the window sill all night — I had a whiff of Peggy Kehoe's cigarette — I was late for school yesterday because I never wanted to go — I was fighting with the lad next door because he tried to take my sweets — and I never went to church on Sunday, Father".

"Why did you not come to church?", asked the priest, in a low gentle voice.

"Because........." "Because what?" continued the priest.

"Well...well it was the money lender", replied Brendon.

"What money lender, what are you saying, my son?". The priest's voice was still low trying to encourage Brendon to continue. "The money lender I killed, she died on Saturday," said Brendon, each word came out in rapid succession.

"I see, so you killed this woman and she died on Saturday, the priest's voice was still low and encouraging. "Are you certain that you carried out this terrible deed?".

"Yes Father" said the panic stricken voice of Brendon.

"Tell me my son, how old are you?". "I'm ten father".

"Your ten years old and you killed the money lender who died on Saturday. Well I think we should start from the beginning, just take your time and tell me what happened?" said the priest.

"Well father it was my bad thoughts that did it".

"Your bad thoughts, is that how the woman died on Saturday! You had bad thoughts and then she died. Did you not like this woman, and do you think that is the reason why she died?" said the priest.

"Yes Father, I wanted her to die and she did", said Brendon, the nervous tension rising in his voice.

"Why did you want her to die?" asked the priest.

"Because she was a money lender, Father".

"Is that all, because she was a money lender? You hoped she would die; what harm had she done to you that you should have such wicked thoughts?" asked the priest, still being very gentle with the boy and his troubled mind.

"She took all my mam's money every week, Father and I would see my mam cry because she had no money".

"And where is your dad, is he at home?" asked the priest.

"No father, he is at sea, me mam said he is brave because he is in the Merchant Navy" said Brendon.

The priest sensed a proud boast from Brendon when he talked about his dad.

"Tell me, where did this woman live who takes all your mother's money each week" said the priest.

"In our street, Father" said Brendon.

"And did the other neighbours borrow money from her?" asked the priest. "Yes Father" replied Brendon.

"And do you think that they have wicked thoughts about her because she was a money lender?" asked the priest.

"I don't know Father".

"You don't know, I see, so do you think perhaps you might have been the only person who would wish to do this woman some harm?", said the priest, his voice still low, still not wishing to panic Brendon.

"I never did her any harm Father", replied Brendon.

"But you did have wicked thoughts about this woman, that's a way of harming people isn't it?" asked the priest.

Brendon fell silent for a few seconds as he shifted himself on the hard wooden seat, "But I never wanted to kill her, I just wanted to stop her taking me mam's money.

She put the money into a big bag, that had lots of other money in it, and sometimes she would count it and while she was doing that she would have a sickly grin on her face, and she would look at me over the top of her spectacles when she was pushing my mam's money into the bag, she looked like an old crow — well me gran said she looked like an old crow".

"Now don't you think that it's wicked describing the woman as an old crow, " said the priest.

"Well me gran thinks she is Father".

"Well I won't argue over that, but its still wrong of you to think that way".

"Yes Father" said Brendon.

"How many brother and sisters do you have?" asked the priest.

"Four sisters and five brothers Father, there's our Mary, our Billy, our Liam," said Brendon, counting them on his fingers, while moving about on the wooden seat.

"I don't want to know their names, and I'm sure that your bad thoughts, as wicked as they were towards this woman, could have been the cause of her death. Do you understand what I am saying to you?" continued the priest.

"Yes Father".

"Then if that's the case go away now and say three Hail Marys two Our Fathers, and offer them up for the repose of the moneylenders immortal soul and God will forgive you, for your sin of bad thoughts providing you have no more wicked thoughts," said the priest.

"Thank you Father".

Impression of a Liverpool side street

12

The Man with the Gaberdine Mack

It's sad the way we make snap judgements on people purely on their physical appearance. A well dressed man or woman can often command respect, whether or not he or she is good, bad or indifferent, a pair of shiny boots will always win the day.

I remember joining a queue of people in a cafeteria in the centre of Liverpool, waiting for my tea and toast. In front of me was a middle aged man and when I saw his shabby and dirty appearance I instinctively stood back so that I would not be in the firing line if he had fleas, in case they wanted to change partners.

He was wearing a greyish gaberdine mack, its true colour had long since faded due to exposure to rain and sunlight over many years.

The structure of his shoes had collapsed leaving the heel of the left lying flat which caused him to shuffle his foot along whilst walking.

After he had been served I watched him make his way to the far side of the cafeteria, and by the time I sat down with my own refreshment I had put him out of my mind.

The following day I called into the same cafeteria for my lunch which was convenient because I was engaged on a job across the road and, standing in front of me was the same man with the shabby mack. He seemed a little cleaner and tidier (by his standards), however, his mack and shoes still had the look of despair about them, his grey hair was shining but his skin still had a healthy look about it even though I could only see the side of his face.

Trying hard to hold my tray steady, my eyes travelled around the cafeteria looking for an empty table or a place to sit.

When at last I found a space at a table, its only occupant was the man with the gaberdine mack. "Do you mind If I sit here?" I enquired.

"Certainly, if you want to, nobody ever sits by me; you must have a pretty low opinion of yourself wanting to sit next to someone like me.

As I sat down I tried not to smile at his comments, as I did not want to show disrespect.

He was surprisingly articulate, the words seemed to flow easily and where crystal clear, his voice had a familiar tone about it, and as I looked into his face, his eyes had a glint that held my gaze.

"How are you *do'in* lad, you don't remember me do you?"
I looked at him across my fish and chips.
"— Oh yes I do — you're Matty Mortimer" I said. surprising even myself at my quick response.
"Are you not having anything to eat", I continued, my voice had a slight tremor through not wanting to offend Matty.
"No, it's alright I have money, I'm not hungry", he gave me a smile that was obviously meant to reassure me.

There was so much that I wanted to ask him, but I was finding a great deal of difficulty in choosing my words.

Matty seemed to understand my inner thoughts and kept on talking about days that had gone, I was content to listen to him, but most of the time, my mind was wandering off, the man sitting facing me was not longer the fit and able young man that I remembered when I was only a youngster.

I don't know why I remembered Matty as quickly as I did when I looked into his face, maybe I was looking into his soul! which was still intact and shone like a beacon to let me see through the well worn face in front of me, to expose the fine and brave young man who had been a local hero in the days of my youth.

Matty seemed to be carried away as he talked about the past, his clear voice was heard by the other diners, his diction was perfect, their heads where swivelled in his direction.

The more he talked about the past the more I recalled mental pictures of Matty on the banks of the Liverpool Canal, he was not a big man but had inner strength. The sight of this man climbing out of the canal as the light faded on a cold January afternoon, being helped by one of the three policemen that stood by — a frantic search had been going on for some hours for a child of four who had disappeared into the black waters.

Matty had been in the water for some time helping with the search, he was handed a blanket by one of the policemen to cover his naked body.

He stood on the pathway only long enough to get his breath back before diving back into the freezing waters once again.

Whenever the alarm went up that a child had fallen into the canal, Matty would be one of the first people on the scene to help the police frogmen.

He would discard his clothes without a word to anybody, then dive into the water as naked as the day he was born.

Quite often only the dead body would be recovered, however,

Matty saved many a youngster who could go on to tell their children, and perhaps grand-children about the man who rescued them.

I can never recall this man receiving a medal or certificate for the many acts of bravery he performed.

Apart from my brief encounter with him when I was at school with his younger brother, I knew very little about him personally other than about his exploits in trying to save children from the canal.

As the banter continued between us at the table it was clear that he knew more about me than I knew about him, and, sitting by Matty had unlocked the gates of our memory.

The more he talked the more other diners turned their heads in his direction, Matty had a pleasant sounding voice that captivated you, its delivery and pitch held you in its power.

The interest of the other diners, the younger ones in particular drew them in days to follow to sit alongside Matty during their lunch break.

Sometimes as many as nine or ten people would be seen sitting with him listening to the wonderful tales he told about his tortourous journey through life.

He talked about his childhood, and he made his misfortunes seem trivial. "I suppose you think I'm hard done by don't you?

Well I might be old and grey and what you would call down on my luck but in truth I'm as free as a bird, I don't live in a cage like a lot of people who only imagine they are free.

Many people burden themselves with all sorts of worries, then go on to say life is hard, but life is what you choose to make it, sometimes we refuse to believe it when things go wrong, it's always somebody else's fault, rarely ever our own.

Most of you will have had a least a cup of tea and a round of toast no matter how much down on your luck you are before you left home this morning".

Matty's young audience listened without interruption, but then a young lady interrupted his flow.
"You tell a fine tale", she said.
"Tale it might be, but just think about it" continued Matty.
"Supposing you lived like most animals in the wild, every day when you awoke you would not have any idea where your next meal was coming from, or even if there was to be a next meal.
Worse still for you, are you yourself to be the next meal for some other animal".

"If you were an animal in the wild you can't go and put the kettle on or get your parents to make you a piece of toast. you would have to go looking for food the minute you opened your eyes.

That takes place every day of their lives, you could be eaten by some other animal looking for their breakfast, or worse still you could be killed by the major predator the human animal who likes to kill just for fun.

Then after spending time in the pursuit of food you return home with food for your young ones who are waiting for your return, because they are hungry.

You find that some other animal has eaten your young ones".

"That tale is a bit depressing Matty", replied another one of his young audience. "Ah! but that's life, so you will have to make sure nobody pushes you out of your nest".

For many weeks I sat, listened and watched Matty entertain his young audience, he was sharp and had an answer for every one of them, with their continual questioning of his life style although they could not hope to fully understand his way of life, they were curious as to why he should be this way. He seemed to be like a lonely white cloud floating, and out of reach to them.

Matty was refreshing to the young people who emerged from stuffy office blocks each day. His world was a way of life that they did not know or understand and, until now, perhaps did not want to, but seeing and listening to him every day made them assess their own values and question them.

While Matty enjoyed the company of the young people each day, he also did not wish for any part of their lives.

His eyes were the focal point with Matty, they drew you to him like magnets that were warm and friendly.

The weeks passed and I, like the rest of the diners who had become acquainted with Matty, looked forward to meeting him each day.

Coming into the cafeteria one day I noticed that Matty was not present, and everybody was eating their meal without a word being exchanged.

When I sat down one of Matty's admirers pushed a local newspaper in front of me, the silence drew my eyes to the page.

"Elderly man found dead in shop doorway.
Covered by a greyish gaberdine mack"

They all missed him dreadfully that I instinctively knew, but, no one present could possibly know just how much I missed him, I could hardly contain my grief — I was one of the children he had saved those many years before and I owed my very life to Matty.

Some pupils and teacher at Martins Camp

13

A pair of shining boots

Joe sat on the side of his bunk, listening to the rest of the young National Service recruits, chatting away, they all seemed a bit nervous in their new surroundings.

Most of the young eighteen and nineteen year olds were trying to put a shine on their new army boots, just one of the first steps they would learn in taking care of themselves.

Joe smiled to himself as he looked down at the black pair of boots perched on his lap, Joe's smile turned into a grin, and his head started to go up and down as though controlled by a spring, his young mind searching as it brushed away the years to when he was eleven years of age.

The boots were the same, but much smaller, Joe could still remember the day that he arrived at Martins Camp during the war years.

Joe alighted from the bus with dozens of other boys, a name tag tied to his lapel displaying his name, age and religion, as Joe walked through the gateway a sign over a small building had the words "All personnel and visitors report here", but there was no sign of life inside the building. Most of the lads tried to look into the windows as they were hurried along.

After walking only a few yards into the Camp the boys were brought to a halt by a kindly looking man who seemed quite old to Joe and the rest of the boys. The ages of the boys were ranged between ten and fourteen, and this man would become known as Daddy Ryan to all who finished up in his class, — not that this place was a school.

The boys had already started talking about the place within minutes of arriving, "this is an army camp", they kept repeating to one another "yes I've seen army camps on the pictures", said one of the older boys, "So have I" said a little ten year old.

"Right lads line up in two's" said Mr. Ryan, "when you are all ready, follow me". Joe and his young comrades were led away to the dining room, clutching the few possessions they had.

Joe listened to the birds that filled the air, he looked up trying to detect their whereabouts, birds of all shapes and sizes, some would sweep low above the marching boys, then climb high into the sky with such speed that the naked eye could hardly follow, Joe would have liked to have named the beautiful birds, but no such birds filled the skies in the worn torn Liverpool he had just left behind.

As Joe and the rest of the boys entered the dining room he could see three men standing at the far end "All come to the front and sit down at the tables", said the taller of the men.

Once seated all the boys were given a glass of milk each.

"While you are drinking your milk I would like to introduce myself, I am your headmaster Mr. Roach and this is Mr. Davies and Mr. Ryan, two teachers who you have already met".

"Well boys I welcome you all to Martins Camp, and I hope you enjoy your stay with us here in the Cheshire countryside" continued the headmaster; and, so began their stay which was for nmost of them was pleasant.

"Come on Scouse get on cleaning your boots, you look like you are day dreaming, thinking about home are you?".
"No" said the startled Joe as he looked at the fresh faced young man sitting facing him, "I was in a place like this when I was only eleven".
"You must be mad" said the young man "You were in an army camp when you were eleven?".

"Yes I was only eleven, all the boys were between ten and fourteen, and we were evacuees from Bootle".

"Where is Bootle?" said the young man with a Lancashire accent.

"It's part of Liverpool".

"I see, so you're from Bootle".

"Yes, but it's Liverpool", continued Joe.

The young man went silent for a few seconds.

"My name's Jimmy Adams, what's your's?"

"Joe, O'Neill"

"Did you really get evacuated to an Army Camp or are you just kidding me?", said Jimmy.

"Yes, I'm telling the truth, and we had pee the beds", said Joe.

"Pee the beds?" said Jimmy with a smile on his face, "What do you mean Pee the beds?".

"Well when we were kids we all had to sleep in double bunks, and if you peed the bed you had to sleep on the bottom bunk, so that way the lad on the bottom bunk would not get wet" said Joe.

"What happened if a lad did pee the bed would he be punished for it?" said Jimmy.

"No, but he had to drag his mattress outside of the billet to dry it out", smiled Joe.

"It must have been a right funny sight seeing all those wet mattresses drying outside", Jimmy was finding the whole thing very amusing.

"It never lasted very long"

"What never lasted very long?" said Jimmy.

"The lads wetting their beds" said Joe.

"Well how did they stop it?".

"They didn't get any milk going to bed", said Joe.

Jimmy looked at Joe waiting for further explanation.

"Every night we would march into the dining room for our supper, every lad knew the place were he had to sit at the long rows of tables running the full length of the dining room.

After being told to stand easy you took your seat and in front of you on the table was a piece of fruit cake and a glass of milk; but in front of the pee the beds there was only a piece of cake without the milk".

Jimmy was looking on in amusement at what Joe was saying.

"How many lads were in your camp"

"About two hundred" said Joe.

"Two hundred lads", said the startled Jimmy, and where you one of the pee the beds?".

"No I was not, do you think I would be telling you if I was one".

"Why not, all lads pee the bed sometime or other".

"I suppose you're right but I was not one of the pee the beds in the camp".

"Sure you're not having me on about this Martins Camp, Joe?".

"No Jimmy I'm telling the truth".

"What was the camp like?".

"It was like this one except that it had bunk beds" continued Joe.

"Yes but it also had pee the beds" said Jimmy with a grin that spread across his round face.

"Do you think there might be a few pee the beds here" continued Jimmy. "Why don't you ask them, but if you do they might wipe that grin off your face".

"What were the teachers like?" said Jimmy.

"They were not bad, most came out of retirement because the war was on, we had one who used to sleep at the end of the billet in his own room, he was there to make sure we never finished up fighting with one another".

"Did you ever get caught fighting?".

"Yes but only once" continued Joe.

"What happened?"

"I had just been to the toilet before lights out, and I was coming back, when another lad twisted my arm as I passed, so I hit him, then the teacher came running out of his room and stopped us from fighting".

"What happened then?" said Jimmy.

"We both got the cane twice on each hand, but I must admit I was more embarrassed than hurt" "Why?" said Jimmy.

Before Joe could answer he blushed.

"Well I was standing in front of the teacher and this lad, and the rest of the billet were hanging out of their beds laughing, while was being caned standing there starkers".

"You mean you had no pyjamas on?" said the amused Jimmy.

"That's right, I didn't even own a pair nor did most of the other lads so we slept in the raw, you had to either have pyjamas on or sleep in your birthday suit".

"I don't think I would have liked that" said Jimmy "but then I never got evacuated. I lived out in the country" he said.

120

"We used to listen to the 'Man in Black' at nine o'clock every week, when we were lying in our bunks".

"Who was the "Man in Black'?" said Jimmy.

"I think his name was Valentine Dyall, and I think it was a sort of ghost story or something like that".

"Some of the lucky lads would be eating sweets and cake, sent from home, most of us would lie there watching them feeding their faces, until lights out".

The banter continued between the two new recruits.

"What happened the next morning did you have to see the headmaster after fighting in the barrack room" said Jimmy.

"Oh no it would be forgotten about, we would be too busy getting dressed and washed to get on to the Parade Ground".

"But why did you have to go on to the Parade Ground?" said a surprised Jimmy.

"We had to be inspected by the headmaster and the teachers".

"Why didn't you go for breakfast first?"

"Because that's what we had to do", continued Joe.

"Every morning was the same, out onto the Parade Ground, then stand to attention, then we would march round, then, after a while we would march over to the dining room for our breakfast. Once outside the dining room we had to stand to attention, then we would march in single file, and we would be in the same order, and go to the same chair every day for our breakfast, dinner and supper. When we all got to our chairs we would be told to stand easy, which meant we could sit down".

"You mean you had to do all that just to get your breakfast?" said Jimmy looking in disbelief, "sure you weren't in Borstal" he said with a smile.

"Well I have never been in such a place, so I would not know what goes in there, perhaps you do?".

"No and I have not been in Borstal either" said Jimmy his hand across his heart.

"Did you enjoy being in Martins Camp?" said Jimmy.

"Yes I suppose we all did, although it was strange for evacuees to be in such a place, there was only one thing that we never like about it", continued Joe.

"Well what was that?" enquired Jimmy.

"It might seem strange to you Jimmy but the Catholics and Protestants never mixed".

"What do you mean, they never mixed? Didn't they like one another", said Jimmy looking up from the chore of polishing his boots.

"Of course they did" continued Joe, "some of my mates were Protestants, but they kept us apart, the Catholics on one side of the camp and the Protestants on the other side, even on the Parade Ground and in the dining room".

"Who was responsible for that Joey-boy?", said Jimmy.

"It's Joe".

"You mean it was you?".

"No I don't mean it was me Jimmy, my name is not Joey-boy it's Joe". "OK, it's Joe but you don't mind if I call you Joey-boy?".

"Alright I give in" protested Joe.

"It must have been some officials in grey suits" continued Joe.

"We even had separate barrack rooms and plots of land".

"What do you mean you had plots of land Joe?".

"Well when we arrived at the camp we were given a little plot of land so we could grow vegetables".

"Did you like growing vegetables?" said Jimmy.

"Yes it was fun, we would go into the fields down the road, and pick the cow dung up with our hands and put it into buckets so we could use it for manure on our plots".

"You mean you would put your hands into cow shit?" said Jimmy with a look of distaste.

"It made good manure" protested Joe.

"Maybe so, but couldn't you have used some other source of manure?".

"We did, we used horse shit, we would follow the horses when they were walking in the country lanes and when they were in the fields".

"Yes and I suppose you still used your hands to put it in the buckets". "We didn't have shovels, so what else could we do Jimmy".

"I don't know but I suppose you would go and eat your dinner after that?". "Yes", said a smiling Joe "but after washing our hands first".

"I would not have liked to have sat next to you in the classroom after you had been on one of your dung gathering exercises. You sure you went to school in Martins Camp?".

"Sure I did I was in Daddy Ryan's class, not that we did much, he would tell us stories most of the time we were in class".

"Were they good stories Joe?".

"Some were true stories, but I think he used to make most of them up".

"Daddy Ryan told us that he was a Seanchai".
"What does that mean, it sounds like a Roman word".
"It's Irish (Gallic) for story teller".
"Could the other teachers tell all sorts of stories?"
"I suppose they could, I can only remember Daddy Ryan teaching us", said Joe.
"I suppose the Sergeant will tell a few tall stories before we finish with National Service and I bet he won't be as nice as Daddy Ryan, he will be more concerned about being able to see his face in my boots", said Jimmy the smile gone from his countenance.

"The camp had a sort of Quarter-Master Store and I think the headmaster had the key to it, you see I remember having holes in my shoes when I first arrived at the camp and I was taken by Daddy Ryan to see the headmaster, who examined my shoes, then he produced this pair of heavy boots from this little storeroom, I thought it was my birthday or something, I had never seen a pair of boots like them".
"Did you have to bull them up the way we are doing ours" said Jimmy who was becoming more interested in Joes' adventure.
"Well not in the same way but we had to be clean and tidy or we would be told about it".
"On a Saturday morning after getting the boots I went into Northwich with the rest of the lads, most of us would buy jars of peanut butter with our pocket money and also metal studs to

hammer into our boots so that we could sound like real soldiers when we went on parade".

"Why did you buy peanut butter?" said Jimmy.

"It was because we could not buy sweets from the shops, they never had any because of the war".

"Do you still like peanut butter Joey-boy?".

"You must be joking I hate the stuff now, I ate so much of it when I was a kid".

Joe's eyebrows came closer together at the thought of the taste of peanut

butter. Jimmy laughed at the distortions on Joe's face.

"Perhaps the Sergeant will let us go down the road for some and that would really make you feel at home Joe".

"I would not eat that stuff now if you paid me".

"Are you sure you are not having me on about this Martins Camp business, I know I am a country lad, and not a Scouser like you, but I'm not daft". "No I am not having you on, it was like an adventure, at least it was when I was only eleven, not that we liked being away from home, far from it, there were times when we would think about escaping and making our own way back home, some of the older lads did manage to get away. The Christian Brothers who managed the camp treated us well but to put a couple of hundred young boys in an Army Camp was not an ideal situation, it was easier on the tougher lads, but for those who had been used to their mams' tucking them up in bed at night it must have been very hard, maybe that's why we had pee the beds in the camp. Just as well we had people like Daddy Ryan in the camp, he must have known how we felt".

Jimmy had forgotten about his boot polishing, how eyes were firmly fixed on Joe.

"Come to think of it Joe, I don't think I am too happy about being away from my girlfriend, I wish she was tucking me up tonight, instead of having to sleep in this billet, listening to this motley crew snoring tonight".

"Never might Jimmy maybe we can get the sergeant to tuck you in".

"Do you think it did you and the rest of the lads any harm?" said Jimmy. "No I don't think so, I suppose in many ways it will help us to encounter some of the knocks life has got in store for us".

"You mean like facing up to this sergeant?".

"I don't think he will do me any harm, although I am not too sure about you, if you don't get those boots bulled up, he might be showing you were to find a big bag of spuds that need peeling".

"I doubt if the sergeant would do that" smiled Jimmy, his manner was beginning to make an impression on Joe. Within minutes of meeting this personable young man Joe was drawn into revealing a chapter in his young life that had lay dormant. Joe's new surrounds in the Army Camp as a National Service man had triggered his thoughts, and Jimmy was the catalyst that brought forth experience that had never been revealed to another living soul.

"The smell is the same Jimmy".

"What smell Joey-boy?" said Jimmy.

"In this place it's the same, you mean from the pee the beds?"

"No, the smell in the Barrack room, even the soap and towels are the same as those we used in Martins Camp, it's the same odour"

"What do you mean Joey-boy, odour?"

"Never mind carry on bulling your boots"

"What other things did you do Joe apart from going to school and marching around the camp like a bunch of boy scouts?".

"The would take us to an assault course, they would say, 'right lads off you go and let's see who gets to the far side first'. So away we would go like March Hares climbing up rope nets, swinging on ropes, running over logs across a stream, then crawling under barbed wire".

"Did they ever lose any of you?" said Jimmy

"Not that I know of" smiled Joe

"When did you eat your sandwiches Joey-boy? Was it while you were impaled on the barbed wire?"

"No I think it was when we were standing on our hands" replied Joe.

"I don't fancy running over an assault course Joe, after all I am a gentle country boy, my father is a Taxidermist" said Jimmy as though it was something to be proud of".

"Yes and my old man is a docker" said Joe.

"And what's a docker?" asked a puzzled Jimmy.

"Well I'll tell you" Joe looked up from the brightness that was starting to radiate from his polished boots. "A docker is a man who works hard he has no time to sit around stuffing birds and animals all day".

Jimmy chose not to comment. "Do you think my boots have attained the required bulling that is demanded by those in charge Joe".

"Well if what you have said just means do your boots have a good shine on them you had better ask Daddy Ryan"

"Who?"

"I mean the sergeant" replied Joe lifting his shining boots.

"This is what the sergeant will be looking for, a pair of shining boots like this".